PRAISE FOR CAN XUE

"Can Xue is one of the most innovative and important contemporary writers in China, and in my opinion, in world literature."—Bradford Morrow

"Can Xue is the most original voice to arise in Chinese literature since the mid-century upheavals. . . . In short, there's a new world master among us and her name is Can Xue."—Robert Coover

"If China has one possibility of a Nobel laureate, it is Can Xue."—Susan Sontag

"Can Xue invites comparison to the century's masters of decay made meaningful, to Kafka especially."
—*New York Times*

"Can Xue's writing is among the most innovative to have appeared in China in recent years."
—*Times Literary Supplement*

"Kafka, Schulz, and Borges. These three are serious company for any author. . . . Can Xue's work is a welcome continuation of their liberating literary projects."
—Matthew Badura, Centre for Book Culture

**ALSO BY CAN XUE
IN ENGLISH TRANSLATION**

VERTICAL MOTION

STORIES

CAN XUE

TRANSLATED FROM THE CHINESE BY
KAREN GERNANT AND CHEN ZEPING

OPEN LETTER
LITERARY TRANSLATIONS FROM THE UNIVERSITY OF ROCHESTER

First edition, 2011
All rights reserved

Several of the stories collected here have been previously published in the
following magazines: "Hongye" [Red leaves], *Shanhua* [Mountain flowers], 2008,
No. 5; "Yefang" [Night visitor], *Xiaoshuo jie* [Fiction world], 1997, No. 4; "Qinglu
shouji" [An affectionate companion's jottings], *Jintian* [Today], 2005, No. 6;
"Dushili de cunzhuang" [A village in the big city], *Furong* [Lotus], 2008, No. 4;
"Alinna" [Elena], *Zuojia* [Writers], 2009, No. 1; "Yueguang zhi wu" [Moonlight
dance], *Shanghai literature*, 2007, No. 1; "Yiyuanli de meiguihua" [The roses at the
hospital], *Shanhua* [Mountain flowers], 2007, No. 8; "Mianhua tang" [Cotton candy],
Zuojia [Writers], 2002, No. 7; "Zijing yuejihua" [The brilliant purple China rose],
Shanghai literature, 2009, No. 2; "Yujing" [Rainscape], *Changjiang wenyi* [Yangzi
literature], 1997, No. 5; "Yong bu ningjing," [Never at peace], *Wenxue shijie* [World
of literature], 1998, No. 5.

Library of Congress Cataloging-in-Publication Data:

Canxue, 1953-
   Vertical motion : short stories / Can Xue ; translated by Karen Gernant
and Chen Zeping. — 1st ed.
      p. cm.
   ISBN-13: 978-1-934824-37-5 (pbk. : acid-free paper)
   ISBN-10: 1-934824-37-2 (pbk. : acid-free paper)
   1. Canxue, 1953–Translations into English. I. Gernant, Karen.
   II. Chen, Zeping, 1953- III. Title.
   PL2912.A5174A2 2011
   895.1'352–dc23
                        2011020159

Printed on acid-free paper in the United States of America.

Text set in Bodoni, a serif typeface first designed by Giambattista Bodoni
(1740–1813) in 1798.

Design by N. J. Furl

Open Letter is the University of Rochester's nonprofit, literary translation press:
Lattimore Hall 411, Box 270082, Rochester, NY 14627

www.openletterbooks.org

To my husband Lu Yong

TABLE OF CONTENTS

VERTICAL MOTION STORIES

We are little critters who live in the black earth beneath the desert. The people on Mother Earth can't imagine such a large expanse of fertile humus lying dozens of meters beneath the boundless desert. Our race has lived here for generations. We have neither eyes nor any olfactory sense. In this large nursery, such apparatus is useless. Our lives are simple, for we merely use our long beaks to dig the earth, eat the nutritious soil, and then excrete it. We live in happiness and harmony because we have abundant resources in our hometown. Thus, we can all eat our fill without a dispute arising. At any rate, I've never heard of one.

In our spare time, we congregate to recall anecdotes of our forebears. We begin by remembering the oldest of our ancestors and then run through the others. The remembrances are pleasurable, filled with outlandish salty and sweet flavors, as well as some crispy amber—the immemorial turpentine. In our recollections, there is a blank passage that is difficult to describe. Broadly speaking, as one of our elders (the one with the longest beak) was digging the earth, he suddenly crossed the dividing line and vanished in the desert above. He never returned to us. Whenever we remembered this, we fell silent. I sensed that everyone was afraid.

Even though people never descended to our underground, we actually gained all kinds of information about the mortals above us. I don't know what sort of channel this information came from. It is said that it was very mysterious, and that it had something to do with our builds. I'm an average-sized, ordinary individual of my genus. Like everyone else, I dig the earth every day and excrete. Recalling our ancestors is the greatest pleasure in my life. But when I sleep, I have some odd dreams. I dream of seeing people; I dream of seeing the sky above. Human beings are good at movement. They feel bumpy to the touch. I'm extremely jealous of their well-developed limbs, because our limbs have atrophied underground. We all move about by wiggling and twisting our bodies. Our skin has become too smooth, easily injured.

We make these kinds of remarks about humankind:

"If you approach the border of the yellow sand, you can hear camel bells ringing: this is what our grandfather told me. But I don't want to go to such a place."

"Human beings reproduced too quickly: it is said that their numbers are immense. They've consumed all of earth's food, and now they're eating yellow sand. It's dreadful."

"If we don't think about the sky and the people on earth, doesn't that ultimately mean that those things don't exist? We have enough memories and knowledge of this kind of thing. It's pointless to go on exploring."

"The yellow sand above us is more than ten meters deep. It's just like the end of the world to those of us who live in the warm, moist, deep soil. I've been to the boundary and have felt the desire to thrust upward. Here and now, I'd like to recall that time."

"Our kingdom of the black earth didn't always exist. It came into being only later. Our oldest ancestors didn't always exist, either. They, too, came into being only later. And so here we are. Sometimes I think that maybe one of us should take a risk. Since we came from nowhere, taking risks is part of our obligation."

"I want to take a risk, too. I've begun fasting recently. I hate my sweaty, damp, and slippery body. I want a change. Whenever I think of yellow sand dozens of meters deep, I'm terrified. But the more terrified I am, the more I want to go to that place. There, I would certainly lose all sense of direction. Probably my only sense of direction would come from gravity. But would gravity change in such a place? I'm very worried."

"We remember all of the history and all of the anecdotes. Why have we forgotten only our long-beaked grandpa? I always feel that he's still alive, but I can recall nothing about him. Recollections concerning each of us are preserved only in our hometown. Once one leaves here, one is thoroughly invalidated by history."

"When I grow quiet, whimsical ideas come into my mind. I would like our collective to ease me into oblivion. Yet, I know this can't be done here. Here, my every word and action will be preserved in everyone's memories, and will be passed on from generation to generation."

"I think I can grow bumpy skin; I just have to make a point of exercising every day. Recently, I've been rubbing and scraping against the rigid clods in the earth. After my skin bleeds, scabs form. It seems this is working."

It's worth pointing out that we critters don't congregate in a certain space for our meetings (as the human beings above us do), for our kingdom of the black earth has no spaces. Everything is packed together. When we do assemble for recreation or discussion, the earth still blocks us off from each other. The black earth is a very good medium for transmitting sound. Everyone can hear every single one of our utterances, even if it's in the feeblest voice. Sometimes while we're digging, we accidentally run into another body. At such times, both sides may feel really disgusted. Ah, we really don't care to have any bodily contact with our own race! It's said that the people above us had to have sexual intercourse in order to propagate: this is much different from our asexual reproduction. Indeed, what does sexual intercourse look like? We don't yet have any detailed information about this. Sometimes when I think of being entangled with my own kind, I start squealing from nausea.

━━━━

When we stop digging, we don't move. We're like pupae as we dream in the black earth. We know that our dreams are similar, but our dreams have never been strung together. Each of us has his or her own dreams. During those long dreams, I can bore deep into the earth and then fuse into a single body with the earth. In the end, my dreams are about only the earth. Long dreams are great, for they are sheer relaxation. But if this goes on for a long time, I feel vaguely discontented, because a dream of earth can never give me the joy that I most want to experience.

Once, we gathered together and talked of our dreams. After I related one of mine, I began crying in despair. What kind of dream was it? It was blacker and blacker until finally it became the black earth. In my dream, I wanted to make a sound, but my mouth had vanished. One after another they consoled me, referring to our ancestors to prove nothing was wrong with our lives. I stopped crying, but something ice-cold settled into my body. I thought it would be difficult to hang onto my previous optimistic attitude toward life. Subsequently, even during working hours, I could feel the heavy black earth pushing down on my heart. Even my rigid beak was weakening, and it itched now and then. I wanted the relaxation that comes from dreaming, but I didn't want the fatigue that comes after waking from a dream. I didn't want to lose interest in life. I must have been possessed. Was I going to disappear in the boundless yellow sand just as our missing ancestor had?

I had recently lost weight, and I was sweating a lot—more than usual. Perhaps because of my mood, I was about to fall ill. When I dug the earth, I heard my companions encouraging me, but for some reason this didn't cheer me up. Instead, I felt sorry for myself and was sloppily sentimental. At break time, an elder talked to me of my late father. He had a lovely buzzing voice, much like the sound sometimes made by the black earth. I called that sound a lullaby. The elder said my father had had a last wish, but he'd been unable to express it. Those beside him didn't probe, either, and thus his last wish hadn't been preserved in our memories. Near death, my father made an odd sound. This old man had been nearest to him, so he heard the sound the most distinctly. He understood immediately that my father wanted to fly like a bird in the sky.

"So did he want to become a bird?" I asked.

"I don't think so. He had a higher purpose."

I talked with the elder for a long time about what my father's last wish might have been. We spoke of sandstorms, of giant lizards, of a certain oasis that had existed, and also of certain minor disturbances involving our ancestors in remote antiquity—because a qualitative change in the earth brought about a scarcity of food. Each time we broached a new topic, we felt we had almost reached my father's last wish. But as we continued talking, it eluded us even more. It really made us uneasy.

Thanks to the elder's information, I gradually calmed down. After all, there *was* a last wish! This made me feel less nihilistic.

"M! Are you digging?"

"Ah, I am!"

"That's good. We've all been worried about you."

These dear friends, associates, kin, and confidants! If I didn't belong to them, who would I belong to? The hometown was so serene, the soil so soft and delicious! I felt that I became a better self. Although my chest still ached dully, the disease had left me. This didn't mean, however, that I was unchanged. I *had* changed. Hidden in me now was an obscure plan that even I couldn't explain.

I was still like everyone else—working, resting, working, resting . . . I heard subtle transformations taking place in our hometown. For example, the tribes decreased in number; the desire to procreate declined; unreasonable complaints spread among us; and so on. Recently, we had begun to amuse ourselves by measuring the lengths of our beaks with the width of our atrophied fingers. "Ha, ha! Mine is three fingers long!" "Mine is four!" "Mine is even longer—four and a half!" Even though our fingers weren't the same width, this activity was still fun for everyone. I discovered that my beak was longer than those of all of my brethren. Was it possible that the elder who had disappeared was my great-grandfather?! Because of my discovery, I broke out in a cold sweat and kept this secret to myself.

"M, how many fingers is your beak?"

"Three and a half!"

I kept my body vertical and continued rushing upward. Everyone soon discovered this change in my motion. I felt the fear all around me. I heard them say: "Him!" "Scary, scary!" "I feel the land wobbling. Will there be an accident?" "M, you need to get hold of yourself." "It isn't in our nature to move straight up!"

I heard all of this. I was engaged in a dangerous activity and couldn't stop this impulse. I ascended, ascended—until, worn out from this work, I slept a dreamless sleep. It was a sound sleep—like death. It was free of confusion and anguish. And I couldn't estimate how long I had slept. After I awakened, my body once more rushed up. This had become a conditioned reflex.

━━

Before long, I noticed a deathly silence all around me; they were probably deliberately staying away from me. Because I was far from the border, others must have been here, too. For the first time in my life, I was alone in an absolutely quiet place. Two large things—black, certainly blacker than the earth—settled over my head all the time. I thought those two things must be heavy and impenetrable. The bizarre thing was that as I kept digging upward, they kept backing off. I couldn't touch them. If I touched them with my beak, would we be together for all eternity? Sometimes, they fused into one huge thing and sometimes they separated again. When they were fused together, they made a *gege* grinding sound; when they were separated, they moaned unhappily. I couldn't think about so many things: I just continued darting ahead as though they weren't there. I thought, *I wasn't supposed to die so soon.* Was I perhaps implementing my father's last wish?

More time passed, and I was working in the deathly quiet and sleeping soundly in the deathly quiet. Scrupulously controlling my feelings so as not to think too much, I knew I was approaching the boundary. Ah, I nearly forgot those two black things! Did I take them to be myself? It was obvious that one could become accustomed to anything. To be sure, I was also sometimes weak, and at such times, I would utter a heartfelt lament: "Father, ah, Father, your last wish is such a terrifying black hole!" This lament gave rise to a misconception: the layers of black earth were twisting me, as if they would twist off my body. I also felt that my ancestors' corpses were hidden in the earth's folds. The corpses emitted spots of phosphorescence. I never hallucinated for very long: I didn't like sentimentality. Most of the time, I ascended step by step. Ascended!

Since beginning vertical motion, I felt that my life was more disciplined—work, sleep, work, sleep . . . Because of this regularization, my mind was also transformed. In the past, I loved to have rambling daydreams—about the layers of black earth, about the ancestors, about Father, about the world above, and so forth. Daydreaming was a way to relax, a kind of entertainment, a kind of tasty turpentine. Now everything had changed. My daydreams were no longer rambling; now they had an objective. As soon as I began resting, those two black things above me started suggesting a direction, and they towed my thoughts in that direction. What was above? Simply those two things. As I was musing, I heard them make the bizarre sound of a watchman's wooden clapper: it was as if someone were striking clappers on an ancient mountain on the ground above and the sound actually reached us underground. Listening attentively, I was thinking of the huge black things. While I was enthralled in this, the sound of the clapper would suddenly stop and become the sound of us insects—many, many insects—boring into the ground. Sometimes I also heard the obscure sound of insects talking—a sound that I seemed to have heard before. Ah, that sound! Wasn't it the very sound that I had heard not long after I split away from my father's body? It appeared that Father was still among us. He brought me a sense of stability, confidence, and a kind of special excitement. A new realm of imagination lay in this. I realized that I liked my present life. When you were about to achieve your objectives, when you incessantly extended your beak toward the things that interested you so much: Didn't you feel happy? To be sure, I didn't think of this too much: I merely felt satisfied with my new circumstances.

I realized tardily that the two black things above were not just totally black, but they contained infinite hues that were in constant flux. The closer I came to the boundary, the weaker and flimsier the core parts seemed to be, as if they would pass through light. Believe me, my body was close to sensing light, which was pink and a little hot. Once, when I overexerted myself, I felt I had torn one of the cores. I even heard a breaking sound—*cha*. I was both excited and afraid. But after a while, I realized that nothing had happened: they were still above me. All was well. I was being silly: How could there be light underground? Now these two things were so exquisite, so seductive. Wasn't Father's obscure voice echoing once again?

Before long, something happened: while I was digging upward, there was a sudden landslide. It was only afterward that I concluded it was a landslide. At the time, I realized only that I was falling and I didn't know where I had fallen. I remember that at first I'd been excited and had faintly heard the noise that was told of in our ancient legends: the sound of people above congregating for singing and dancing. At the time, I thought, *How can there be a congregation in the desert?* Or perhaps it wasn't a desert over us, after all? Now, the two black things above me really did let light through. I am speaking merely of my conclusion, because I wasn't aware of it. This light wasn't pink, nor was it yellow or orange. It was a thing that you couldn't sense, wedged between the two black things. The sound of the musical accompaniment became increasingly intense, and I grew increasingly excited. I exerted all of my strength to thrust upward . . . and then there was the landslide.

I was despondent, for I thought I had certainly fallen to the place where I was before I started my vertical motion. But a long time passed, and silence still lay all around me. Did another kingdom lie beneath the desert, a dead kingdom? It was very dry here, and the earth was not the black earth of before. All of a sudden, it came to me: this wasn't earth, it was sand! Right. This was shapeless sand! I had clearly fallen down, so how had I ended up in this kind of place? Could gravity have changed direction? I didn't want to think about this too much. I had to start my work as soon as possible, for it was only work that could put me in a good mood with a steady self-confidence.

I began digging—still in the upward, vertical motion. Motion in the desert was quite different from motion in the earth. In the earth, you could sense the track—and the sculpture—your motion left behind. But this heartless sand submerged everything. You couldn't leave anything behind, and so you couldn't judge the direction of your motion. Of course, with my present lifestyle, vertical motion was just fine, because my inner body was attuned to gravity. As this went on, I felt that this work was harder and tenser than before. And what I ate was sand: flavor was out of the question. I ate it just to fill my stomach. I was tense because I was afraid of losing my direction by mistake. I had to keep paying attention to my sense of gravity: it was the only way to maintain the vertical route. This sand would seemingly choke all of my senses. I had no way to know if I was even in motion. And so my feelings shrank inward. There was no longer a track, not to mention the sculpture, but only some blurred throbbing innards, along with flashes of faint light in my brain.

And so, was I squirming in the same spot or was I moving up? Or sinking down? Was I capable of determining this? Of course not. Every so often I made expanding and contracting motions, which I thought meant I was moving up. Of course the sand's resistance was not nearly as great as the earth's, but this slighter resistance left me uneasy. If you have nowhere to stand, then you have no way, either, to confirm the results of your exertions, and there's likely to be no result. After tiring from my activity, I ate some sand and then fell into a death-like sleep. After my skin cracked, it healed again, and after healing it cracked again. Little by little, it was thickening. The humankind above me wears thick skin. Had they all gone through what I was experiencing? Ah, this quiet, this desolation! One can probably endure it for a short time, but if it persists, isn't it the same as being dead? Uneasiness germinated tardily in my mind. I reflected on the one who had disappeared: Perhaps he was still alive? One possibility was that he and I were both living and that we would never actually die. Buried by this boundless yellow sand, each of us leapt on his own, and we would never be able to see each other. When I considered this possibility, I began twitching all over. This occurred a number of times.

The last time it happened, it was really dreadful. I thought I would die. I became aware of the mountain, which was the two black things that had formerly been above me. After disappearing for a time, they had returned. They pressed down toward me, but didn't press me to death. They were just suspended above. At this time, I stopped having spasms at once. As this eased, at first my consciousness functioned rapidly, and then it was entirely lost. I leapt up with all my strength! At once, the mountain weakened so much that it was like two leaves—leaves of the phoenix tree above ground. Indeed, I sensed that they were drifting. As I saw it, a miracle was taking place. In my excitement, I leapt again, and now there were four phoenix leaves! There were actually four. I heard the sound of each one. It was the metallic sound mentioned in legends. I knew I hadn't lost my way: I was on the correct path! Soon, the metallic leaves would split and I would see light! Although I had no eyes, this wouldn't preclude my "seeing." I—an insect underground—would see light! Ha ha! Not so fast. How would I do this? With my scarred, haggard, restless body? Or was it just my mirage? Who could guarantee that the instant I emerged from the earth wouldn't be the moment of my death? No, I didn't want to get to the bottom of this question. It would be fine if I could just keep sensing the phoenix leaves above me. Ah, those eternal metallic leaves: the cool breeze on Mother Earth shuttled among the leaves . . .

I fainted. When I came to, I heard sand buzzing all around me, and in this sound an old, low voice spoke:

"M, is your beak still growing?"

Who was it? Was it he? Who else could it be? So much time had passed. This desert, this desert . . . How could things be like this?

"Yes, my beak, my beak! Please tell me: Where am I?"

"You're on the uppermost crust of the earth. This is your new home."

"Can't I bore my way out of it? Are you saying that from now on I can only wander around in this sand? But I'm accustomed to vertical motion."

"You can only engage in vertical motion here. Don't worry, there's more sand on top of this sand."

"Are you saying I cannot break out completely? Oh, I see. You've tried it. How long have you lived in this region? It must be a very long time. We can't measure the time, but we know we lost you long ago. Dear ancestor, I never imagined, never imagined that in this—how to say it?—that in this extremity, I would come across you. If my father . . . ah, I can't mention him. If I do, I'll faint again."

He didn't say any more. I heard his far-off voice: *cha, cha, cha* . . . as he dug the sand with his long, senile beak. My bodily fluids were boiling. It was bizarre: I'd stayed in such an arid place for so long and yet I still had fluids in my body. Judging by the sound I heard, this ancestor had fluids in his body, too. This was really miraculous! Somewhere above me, he walked away. He must have seen the phoenix leaves, too.

Ah, he returned! How wonderful—now I had a companion! I had someone to communicate with. The boundless yellow sand was no longer so frightening! Who . . . who was he?

"Grandpa, are you the one who disappeared?"

"I am a wandering spirit."

This was great: I spoke, and someone answered me. How long had I been without this? Someone of the same species would engage in the same activity and live with me in this desert . . . Father's last wish was for me to find him: I realized this!

———

I was a little critter submerged in the desert. This was the outcome I had pursued. In this mid-region, I was envisioning the phoenix leaves on Mother Earth. Yet, I didn't forget my kindred in the dark.

RED LEAVES

The first light of morning had just streamed through the sickroom's window. Teacher Gu lay on the bed with his eyes closed. The cleaning woman was spraying disinfectant in the room. She had arrived particularly early today, as though coming not to clean but to disturb him. Gu knew he couldn't go back to sleep, for each time this happened, his thoughts leapt up in the midst of the strong smell of Lysol. One red leaf floated in the air above the forest of his thoughts—a forest that was totally bare, for it was winter now. Gu had been pondering a question for several days: Did a leaf start turning red from the leaf-stalk, the color gradually spreading throughout the entire leaf, or did the entire leaf gradually turn from light red to deep red? Before falling ill, Gu hadn't observed this phenomenon, probably because he missed the chance every year. In front of his home were hills where maples grew. But it was only after he fell ill that he had moved there.

After the cleaning woman left, Gu bent his legs and lightly massaged his distended belly. He thought: *perhaps one's body is most vibrant when one's disease reaches its last stage. His poor liver, for instance, must have reached this stage.* A tragedy had occurred last night in this large ward: a terminally ill patient had rushed with a roar to the balcony and jumped. After that, the ward was as still as death, as though no one lying there dared utter a sound. Was it because someone had died that the cleaning woman had come so early to disinfect the room? He thought this was unreasonable. The person hadn't killed himself because his condition had worsened and his pain was unbearable. He knew he was improving after going through chemotherapy. The next day he would have been moved out of the ward for serious cases. Who could have guessed that he would do this? This guy really chose an original approach.

After staying in the hospital for a long time, Gu was more and more content with his situation. In private, he even praised the hospital as "fascinating." He was a taciturn patient, accustomed to being moved around along the corridor that connected the white structures. Actually, he could walk slowly by himself, but the doctors insisted that he use a wheelchair. He sat in a wheelchair, and a big fellow pushed him carefully to the treatment room. Gu thought this arrangement was actually intended to prevent him from escaping. At first, he thought this was suspicious, but later he grew accustomed to it and even understood it a little. The next time he was in the wheelchair, he imagined that he was a general making a leisurely inspection of a battlefield littered with corpses.

He was resting with his eyes closed when he suddenly heard the cleaning woman say: "As the man jumped, he was shouting Mr. Gu's name." When he opened his eyes, he saw the cleaning woman turn and leave the room. Her words agitated Mr. Gu. For some reason, all at once his hearing became extremely acute: once again, he heard two people talking on the top floor. They walked downstairs, arguing about something. As they made their way from the ninth floor to the seventh floor and then to the sixth floor, their voices grew louder, as if they were quarreling. They stopped on the sixth floor. They then lowered their voices, and the quarrel turned into a discussion. They sounded like two cats mewing softly. Gu's room was on the fifth floor. The two people would have to descend only one more floor and they'd be at his door. But they didn't. They stood up there and kept talking. Their language became completely distorted. The more he heard, the more it sounded like cats meowing. The word "catmen" appeared in his mind, and he even imagined that many "catmen" were in this hospital. They hid in dark corners and sometimes emerged to confide their loneliness in someone, just as they were doing now. The right side of his belly throbbed a few times, and he heard the fluids gurgle there. He closed his eyes and saw the red leaf again. The edge of the leaf had thickened and was imbued with a bizarre fleshy sensuality. Gu felt something flicker in his head. One of the "catmen" suddenly gave a loud shout before his voice became inaudible. The door opened. Breakfast had arrived.

Gu wasn't hungry and didn't want to eat. Lei, the patient next to him, urged him: "Have a little. If an incident like that is repeated tonight, you'll need some energy to deal with it." Lei was in the last stages of his disease. He'd lost his hair long ago and had only a month or two to live. After thinking it over, Gu reluctantly sipped a little milk and rinsed his mouth with water. Holding back his nausea, he lay down again. He noticed that Lei was in high spirits as he ate his egg. This person?? How come? He wanted to talk with Lei about the "catmen," but he felt too weak to talk. Last night, why had the accountant Zheng shouted his name as he jumped? It was a little like toying with him. At this point, he subconsciously raised one hand, but then he heard Lei saying:

"Mr. Gu, don't ward it off with your hand. Let it fall on your face. Maybe it will be hypnotic."

"What?!" He was shocked.

"I'm talking of the small leaf. Look, it fell onto your quilt. Ha!"

Sure enough, there *was* a withered leaf on his quilt. It had come in through the window. When he twisted the leaf lightly, it crumbled into powder. The powder stuck to his hand, so he shook it off. Then he wiped his hands clean with a handkerchief. His eyes half-closed, he leaned against the pillow and heard the consulting doctors enter the room. Under the doctors' questioning,

Lei appeared unusually happy and answered their questions loudly. He declared that he had "conquered the disease." Through the slits of his eyes, Gu observed the disgusted frown of the physician in charge. Gu thought, "Lei will die soon. Perhaps tonight?" Suddenly, Lei uttered, "Ouch," and Gu opened his eyes.

He saw several doctors pressing Lei down onto the bed. He resisted vehemently, but they still bound him to the bed with strong tape. He was yowling through it all, and it looked as if his bulging eyes might jump out of their sockets. The doctors pulled out handkerchiefs to wipe away their perspiration and appeared to breathe sighs of relief. For some reason, they didn't approach Gu, but went to the two beds on the west side of the room. After asking questions for a while, they left the ward. Their unusual behavior made Gu's brain alternately tighten and turn blank. After a while, Lei vomited blood. It fell onto his face and then streamed onto the pillow. The blood was blackish-red. He no longer struggled, nor could he struggle. Now he could move only his mouth, eyes, and nose. No. His ears, too. Gu noticed that his ears were moving, making him look as cute as an animal.

"Lei, let's just take it easy" Gu found something to say.

"You————idiot!" he said.

Gu fell silent. The right side of his belly pulsed again, and he patted it. It throbbed even more. With waves of heat gushing in, he began feeling feverish. In the west part of the room, wardmates—a man and a woman—compared notes on cemetery reservations. Their meticulous, earnest attitude made Gu shiver with cold. Feeling partly hot and partly cold, he touched those spots and said softly, "This isn't like my body." He secretly intended to slip out after a while and look for those "catmen." Ordinarily, he didn't dare leave the ward, because as soon as he left, Lei would push the call button and he'd be hemmed in by nurses.

Gu got up stealthily and, making his way along the wall, left the room. At the doorway, he looked back and saw Lei glowering at him. This suddenly struck him as quite funny, and he almost laughed. At this time, the corridor was empty, and he stole over to the staircase and quietly went upstairs. As he climbed the stairs, he held his paunch with both hands and imagined that he was a kangaroo.

When he reached the sixth floor, he heard the "cat language." But where were the "catmen"? No one was on the sixth floor corridor except for two nurses making their rounds with medications. After a moment's rest, Gu continued climbing up. On the seventh floor, a worker delivering water was pushing his small cart. He stopped at the edge of the corridor and sat on the stairs to smoke a cigarette. Gu wondered how he could smoke near the wards. The person patted the floor next to him and invited Gu to sit down and have a cigarette with him. Surprised, Gu accepted his cigarette and a light. The cigarette was very strong. Gu had never seen this brand before; perhaps he had rolled it himself. Then he noticed that the cigarette case was plastic.

"You know how to roll your own cigarettes," Gu commented admiringly.

"My buddies . . . We have the right tools . . ." he answered vaguely.

After finishing the cigarette, Gu thanked the worker and stood up, intending to continue up the stairs, when he suddenly heard the worker beside him make a cat sound. It was very harsh. But when he glanced at him, he looked as if nothing had happened. No one else was here. If he hadn't made the sound, who had? Gu changed his mind; he wanted to see if this person would do anything else.

He waited a while longer, but the worker didn't do anything; he just put his cigarette butt in his pocket, rose, and went back to the water cart. He pushed the cart into the ward. Gu subconsciously put his hand into his own pocket, took out the cigarette butt, and looked at it, but he saw nothing unusual. In a trance, he twisted and crushed the butt. He saw an insect with a shell moving around in the tobacco threads. The lower half of its body had been charred, but it still didn't seem to want to die. Nauseated, Gu threw the butt on the floor and, without looking back, climbed to the eighth floor.

Everything was in a hubbub in the eighth floor corridor, where there were a lot of people. Probably someone's condition had worsened, for he saw a cart of instruments being pushed into the ward. After resting for a moment, Gu started up to the ninth floor—the top floor.

When he had almost reached it, he looked up and was so startled that he nearly fell down the stairs. A person clothed all in black and wearing a ferocious opera mask stood there, looking as though he were waiting especially for Gu.

"Hello, Mr. Gu!" he said in a loud voice, as harsh as a chapel gong.

Gu sat on the floor, gasping for breath and unable to speak. Suddenly, he felt tired and his belly began aching. It seemed that no patients were on the ninth floor, so the corridor was empty. Gu wondered which room the "catmen" were in. Was this masked person a "catman," too?

"I was your student!" the masked person said loudly. "I'm Ju—the one who jumped into the icy river to save someone. Have you forgotten?"

"You're Ju? Take off your mask and let me look at you. So you didn't disappear, after all!"

He took off the mask, and Gu saw the pale face of a middle-aged man who was a stranger to him. How could he be the Ju who had jumped into the icy river to save another person and then disappeared? That had been a warm-hearted boy. Something was wrong with this middle-aged man's eyes; there was a film on them—probably cataracts. But never mind: Gu felt quite emotional about encountering a student he had liked in the past.

"I've been looking for you all these years, and not long ago, I finally ran into someone who knew where you were. He said you were hiding out here. This place is really concealed!"

Ju took Gu's arm and said he wanted to go into a room to talk. They went into a ward and sat on the beds. It was dark with the blinds closed. Gu started coughing because of the dust raised from the bed. Puzzled, he wondered how long it had been since someone had stayed in this room. Ju sat on the bed opposite his. When Gu looked up to take stock of him, this middle-aged man seemed to have turned into a flimsy shadow. Gu watched him writhing as he lay down, lifted up the dusty quilt, and covered himself. Gu started coughing hard again.

"I'm so lucky," he said, "to be in the same room with the teacher I loved and respected. Please sit on my bed and put your hand on my forehead, okay? I've been dreaming of this for a long time."

When Gu placed his right hand on Ju's forehead, his own body trembled as if an electric current were running through it. It was plain to see that this person really was Ju! Back then, he and Ju had been chasing a red leaf up to the cliff, talking along the way. Seen from the top of the cliff, their high school had looked like blackened scars on trees. It was that day that Gu had told Ju of his own unmentionable disease.

When someone knocked a few times on the door, Gu wanted to get up and open it, but Ju held him back.

"Who could it be?" Gu said.

"Ignore it. It's those doctors. They knock a few times to confirm that no one is here and then they leave."

Sure enough, Gu heard several persons' footsteps going down the stairs.

"Don't you find it hard to lie down in all of this dust?" Gu asked Ju.

"It's wonderful here, Mr. Gu! Would you put your hand on my

forehead again? Ah, thanks so much. It's so peaceful here that three roosters are running over."

Gu strained to recall what they had talked about back then and finally remembered. Ju had also divulged his own unmentionable disease. He told him there'd been a hole in his chest since birth and his heart protruded from that hole. He could see his own heart beating. Ordinarily, he covered the hole with gauze and then taped it in place. He confided to Gu that he didn't feel this defect was a major handicap, and he also added innocently, "Look, I get along fine, don't I?" Later, he jumped into the icy river and didn't emerge. So was it just on a pretext that he had come to the hospital? Was the real reason that his life was also nearing its end?

"When I lived next to the maple forest, where were you?"

"Me? I was in the forest!"

Ju suggested that Gu lie down too, and so Gu did. When he covered himself with the dusty quilt, a thread of pleasure germinated in his heart. He heard a sound from his fifth-floor room: a group of doctors and nurses were looking for something there. Ah, were they looking for Lei? They said that Lei, who had been tied to his bed, had disappeared. Not only this, but Lei had also pulled a prank: he had tied a piglet onto the bed. He was really devilish! Gu heard not only the doctors' conversations but also the very familiar meows coming from the fifth floor corridor. Gu thought the meows were coming from a "catman." That "catman" was with him day and night. Could Lei be a "catman"? Or had those "catmen" set Lei free? Gu looked around the large ward and was surprised by the desolation. When he was downstairs, he always thought the top floor was very busy; it was even more possible that those "catmen" were hiding here. The other day, he had sat in the wheelchair and an aide had pushed him to the flat roof on the ninth floor. At the time, he thought he was about to die. The big fellow pushed the wheelchair around the periphery of the flat roof and told him to look down. He looked a few times: muddy waves were all around. Then he heard all kinds of screams coming from everywhere in the building, as if the end of the world had arrived. Still later, grumbling and swearing, the big fellow took him downstairs and pushed him into his own ward. At the time, five other patients were still in the room. As soon as he entered, everyone rose respectfully and looked at him with envious eyes. One of them—a young person named Bei Ming—said, "This is like winning the lottery!" His entire day floated amidst everyone's compliments.

"Mr. Gu, have you seen my mask?" Ju said. "I must have left it on the stairs. Without it, I can't see anyone except for you."

Gu thought for a long time, but he couldn't figure out why Ju had to wear a mask to see people. He really wanted to ask him what he had experienced after he disappeared, but he could never broach the subject. He thought it would be the same as asking his student: "After you died, where did you go? What unusual things did you see?" He just couldn't do it. He slowly massaged his fluid-filled belly, and his thoughts flew to the beginning stages of his disease. He'd felt then as if a load had been taken off his mind. In high spirits, he had moved to the slope at the maple forest and had spent some lovely days there. In the autumn, the red leaves had intoxicated and entranced him. He'd never felt so sensitive to the world around him as he did then. In his excitement, he even saw eagles. Autumn was a long season. He said to himself: "Autumn is so long—like eternal life." Sometimes, old friends came to see him, but they weren't the one he wanted to see. Back then, he couldn't think who it was that he wanted to see. Only now, lying here, did he know. The one he had wanted to see all along was this student who had disappeared. As he thought of this, the fluids in his belly made a pleasing sound, and a grateful sensation spread throughout his body.

Gu heard them free the Dutch piglet that Lei had tied to the bed. As soon as the piglet was freed, it scurried out of the ward. The people garbed in large white gowns looked at each other in dismay. Someone said softly, "This never would have occurred to me." But Gu thought, *Perhaps this had occurred to them some time ago.* Nothing could easily defeat someone like Lei. Even the person who jumped from the window the night before had ordinarily done as Lei said.

Ju was snoring comfortably in the next bed. Gu thought, *He's so at peace with himself that even the clamor in the building can't disturb him.* Gu really wanted to learn how far Ju's disease had progressed. He intended to ask him as soon as he woke up. Gu had seen Ju jump into the icy river, but he couldn't ask him how he had been revived after his bare heart had been submerged in the icy water. He merely wanted to ask about his present condition. His face had always been as white as limestone, and it still was. From looking at him, it was impossible to guess how bad his condition was. He felt that although his appearance had changed, he was still as gentle as before. Perhaps it was because he could see his own heart that he had been so sure about what he was doing—for instance, jumping into the icy water.

"Ju, let's go to see the red leaves next year, okay?" Gu said to the air.

A meow came in from the door: it was Lei talking with someone. Of course Lei was a "catman." It seemed three people were outside: Why didn't they come in? The big white gowns from the fifth floor were also heading upstairs, but neither Lei nor the others paid any attention to the doctors. Gu heard them say that doctors were "garbage."

After the doctors came upstairs, they didn't encounter Lei and the others. Gu heard them plotting something—something that Gu was very familiar with, something that he had once participated in but had completely forgotten. What was it? Gu felt unable to express it in words. When this group entered the opposite ward, they closed the door, nipping the Dutch piglet's leg in the process. The piglet howled. Someone turned around, freed the curious little pig, and let it in.

Gu groped under his pillow for a flashlight; probably a former patient had left it there. Feeling excited, he immediately walked to Ju's bed with the flashlight. Seeing that he was still sound asleep, he lifted the quilt and shone the flashlight on his chest. Ju's torso was bare, and so Gu immediately saw his pulsating heart. For some reason, his heart was the color of milk. It beat much slower than most people's. Peering through the hole, he saw that the beating heart was shifting its position. This baffled him.

"This is just the way my heart is, Mr. Gu." Ju opened his eyes and spoke apologetically.

"Ju, can you hear the secret meeting in the ward across the way? What are they discussing?"

Ju took hold of the flashlight and shone it toward the door. Gu also turned his gaze in that direction. A doctor was standing there, but he wasn't one of the doctors who made rounds. Gu had never seen him. The doctor blocked the flashlight's rays with his left hand and said: "It's good to be here. We're prepared for an emergency at any moment."

Then he left, closing the door behind him. Ju laughed softly and commented that this hospital was "quite interesting." He put on his black jacket and his opera mask. Gu asked him where he had found the mask, and he said that actually he hadn't lost it: he'd forgotten that it was at his waist all the time. After he dressed, he told Gu that he wanted to go across the hall "to take part in the meeting." Gu—heart thumping—went with him. He had a hunch that the truth would come out. His hands began trembling.

When Ju appeared in the room wearing the opera mask, everyone's head swiveled in his direction. The blinds were all open, so it was quite light, and Gu noticed that neither Lei nor the doctors were there. They were all his closest friends and relatives, but he couldn't recall any of their names.

Someone pushed a wheelchair out, and Gu thought it was for him. He never imagined that Ju would beat him to it. Sitting in the wheelchair, Ju looked happily inebriated. Gu begrudged him the wheelchair, because he usually used it. Two big fellows were pushing Ju, and Gu thought they intended to leave the room, so he quickly made way for them. But they didn't go out; they just pushed the wheelchair around in the empty ward. Ju grabbed at something in the air. He looked absorbed, and the people around him were cheering him on. Just then, Gu glanced out the window: what he saw was the splendid spectacle of drifting red leaves. Astonished, he sat down on the floor. How could there be red leaves in the winter? In the sunlight, the leaves were like flames.

Now—with Gu at the end of the line—everyone was following the wheelchair as it made the rounds in the room. The footsteps sounded like marching. As Gu listened attentively, he even felt that everyone's footsteps were lost in thought. Walking and walking, Gu no longer looked out the window, because a shadow was filling this circle. Everyone was sinking into this dense, dark shadow. At last, Ju plucked something from the air. He took off his mask and smelled the thing.

"Mr. Gu! Mr. Gu! This is it!" He seemed to be weeping.

"What is it, son?" Gu asked.

"It's the thing I jumped into the river for!"

All of a sudden, the people's footsteps were no longer in sync. In the dense, dark shadow, Gu couldn't get a good look at these faces, nor could he see the scenery outside the window. But he could still hear Ju calling him and he could still hear the wheelchair rolling past. The two big fellows had vanished, and the wheelchair was being steered automatically. A dark gust of wind in the room took hold of him and detached him from the circle. In the corridor, Gu still heard Ju shouting: "Mr. Gu! This is it!!"

When Gu went downstairs, the entire building rang with all sorts of meows. They were meowing wildly everywhere—in the wards, the offices, and the bathrooms. Gu knew they weren't cats but were "catmen" hiding in this building. Perhaps they'd been provoked by Ju's arrival. He himself had stayed here such a long time, and yet they'd never gone wild like this before. Ju must be the key character. If he hadn't come, the "catmen" might have merely been a little restless. And the red leaves wouldn't have appeared outside the window in winter. He quickly went down to the fifth floor, where the odor of Lysol made him drowsy. He thought, *The person who jumped from the ward window last night: perhaps the words he had shouted were identical to the words Ju had just shouted—"Mr. Gu! Mr. Gu, this is it . . ."*

"Everyone has to die. After death, there's nothing." My late father once said to me, "After you die, who knows what you had planned while you were alive?" Having said this much, he lifted his head arrogantly. A nearly despicable expression floated across his face.

After hearing this, I remember glaring at him a few times and sneering inwardly twice. As for him, he strolled around the room. He was wearing a pair of old-fashioned shoes, and his nylon socks gave off a sour, sweaty smell. That smell permeated the room all summer, for he never opened windows.

Father's bedroom was at the end of the house; when he went out, he had to go through all of our rooms, but we didn't need to go through his room. I went to see him about once a month. He generally closed his door and kept busy as a mouse with his large pile of old books. When I knocked, he was flustered when he came to the door. As he covered what he was working on, he led me around a large stack of disorganized books and settled me into an old chair beneath the window. The cushion, made of yellowing reed catkins, was lumpy and uncomfortable. When he and I talked, he blocked my line of vision with his broad body. Perhaps he was afraid that I'd see what he was working on.

At the time, I regarded Father as an old man with nothing to do, a person who lingered on in a worsening condition in a dark room. Family members and neighbors thought the same thing. Because he'd been retired for years, you could say that he had retired from life a long time ago. Generally, no one thought much about him. Sure, he had a few foibles. You couldn't say he was sick just because he liked staying in his room and not going out. Old people always take things to extremes.

━━━

It was time for me to visit Father again. I was a little concerned, because he hadn't eaten much for a few days and he wasn't in a good mood, either. He was always angry, scolding people at the dinner table for no reason. Everyone was baffled by this. When he opened the door, his thin face was expressionless. I glanced into the room: he'd covered all the books with an old cloth, and the old chair had been moved away from the window. Father didn't seat me while we talked. He was standing, too, because—apart from that old chair—the only place to sit was a small stool. Ordinarily, he sat on it to straighten out his heap of old papers, but this time, for whatever reason, he had tucked the small stool under the bed.

I stood there chatting aimlessly of household trivia. As I talked, I was getting more and more flustered, for all I wanted was to escape from there as soon as possible and steer clear of this awkward errand in the future. Through all of this, Father kept a straight face and paced with his hands behind his back. All of a sudden, he stopped, walked over, and shoved open a side door that faced the courtyard. The room brightened at once. Only then did I notice that he had moved the cupboard and begun using the side door behind it that had been closed for years. The door had warped, requiring great strength to open it, and it was even harder to close again. Father beckoned to me to help him.

We pushed it hard several times before it reluctantly closed. As I brushed the dust from my clothes, I noticed that his haggard face was a little flushed.

"Rushu, you never thought I could open this door, did you?" Father turned around so that I couldn't see his expression. "This door goes straight to the courtyard. Something could happen without anyone knowing. Of course the rest of you wouldn't notice, for you're preoccupied with other things. Your attention wanders, and so does your sister's."

"Papa—" I said.

"One can do whatever one wants to do!" He twisted around crabbily and looked at me almost savagely. "Do things furtively, and no one knows. Ah!"

"Papa, if you feel bored staying here alone, you could take walks in the park with me every day," I said uncertainly.

"Me? Bored? Whatever made you think that? Let me tell you, I'm a very busy man." With that, looking extremely arrogant, he seemed to start thinking intently about something.

"Rushu, get me the scissors from the lowest drawer," he ordered.

I felt that at this moment Father was extremely vigorous. It was as though he wanted to strut his stuff over something.

The drawer was a jumble of little sundries. After searching for a while, I found the small scissors and handed them to him.

Taking the scissors, he charged over to where he usually sat, removed the old cloth, grabbed an old book, and began carefully snipping the book into scraps. In this dim room, the *kaki kaki* sound of the scissors was particularly grating. I could hardly control my feelings.

After cutting up one book, he cut up another. There were not only books in the pile, but also all kinds of old notes and correspondence. He cut whatever he got hold of. After a while, the floor was stacked with wastepaper. I saw his old bare, blue-veined hand squeezing the scissors hard. His fingernails turned purple. When he wasn't paying attention, I quietly withdrew to the doorway.

"Rushu, go ahead and leave. There's nothing here that concerns you," he said from behind me.

———

It was about a week later when I heard my colleagues' rumors about my family members and me mistreating my aged father. They made special mention of me, saying that I "had cut Father's palm with scissors" and that Father "had wailed." The rumors were well-founded and vivid, and I couldn't help shuddering. I didn't dare look at the others, nor did I dare defend myself. I just shivered blindly.

It was tough to endure this until I got off work. When I reached home, I groped for my key in my purse in the dark corridor. Just then, my brother leapt out from an invisible place and patted me on the shoulder. Paralyzed with fright, I nearly fell to the ground.

"Ha ha!" He patted me on the shoulder again and said with a laugh, "You got off work really early today."

"Early? It doesn't seem early to me." I looked at him bitterly. I wanted to go to my own room.

"It *is* early." He yanked on my arm and continued talking. "It's hard for all of us siblings to get together. Usually everyone is busy. We only sit at the same table at mealtimes. Although we sit together, we don't talk much. I think this is because Father is present. Looking at him, who dares talk and laugh freely? As I see it, when one is old, one should know one's place and retreat from life. Paternalistic behavior won't do him any good in the end. Sometimes, I can't avoid thinking that this family isn't a family anymore! It's oppressive, disorganized, and unreasonable. Do any other families maintain patriarchy as we do?"

"You've been dismissive of Father for a long time, haven't you? Why are you being so alarmist?" I interrupted him in disgust.

"That's the way it is on the surface. You're the same. Behind his back, we say he's a piece of old garbage. Everyone seems to ignore him. But do we truly ignore him? At the table, I've noticed your knees trembling."

I threw his hand off and entered my room in one stride.

When we ate dinner, Nishu talked of the encephalitis that was rampant in other towns. She rapped her chopsticks on the table for emphasis. I sneaked a look at Father and saw that he was looking down wretchedly, preoccupied with his worries. After pushing a few bites of food into his mouth, he set his bowl down and stood up to leave.

"Papa didn't eat a thing!" I said loudly. "Look, he hasn't eaten anything for days!"

All of us put our chopsticks down and looked at Father in consternation.

Nishu seemed chagrined and said accusingly: "What's wrong with you, Papa?"

Apparently his old self again, Father stared at everyone, and looking haughty, he held his head high and returned to his room.

Something was collapsing in my heart. I recalled the door that Father had quietly opened in his room, and I couldn't help feeling misgivings. I thought that my colleagues' rumors were connected with that door. Why? Because Father abhorred outsiders entering his room, and so twenty years ago he had sealed off the door that opened onto the courtyard. Previously, when he burrowed single-mindedly into the pile of old books, I didn't have to worry. What kind of elderly person's crazy idea had led him to take this step? It would be difficult to tell someone like Father to retreat entirely from life. He'd been quiet for years and hadn't made any trouble. Now, when everyone was almost accustomed to this, this awkward situation had suddenly cropped up. Maybe we didn't really understand Father. Perhaps, during these years, he'd been making preparations all along. Perhaps the inflated illusions in his head had caused him to lose his common sense.

My colleagues' rumors didn't subside. I felt pressure from all directions. With every passing day, this pressure made me feel more and more dread and disgust. I thought it over and made up my mind to confront Father. I would catch him off guard and see how he explained his behavior. I was vexed and unhappy. I couldn't figure out why he had to cause so much trouble.

When it had just turned dark, I hid in the oleander grove in the courtyard. Father stood in front of the window, his shadow reflected on the curtains. His back was stooped. I thought of his face that had become increasingly thin, and I felt something that I couldn't express. After a while, he bent his head, as if to cut his fingernails and also as if he was fiddling with his watch. About half an hour later, he covered the light with a newspaper. When I looked across, it was as if he'd blacked out the light and gone to sleep. I knew he wasn't asleep, for I heard him sighing quietly. I sat on the small stool I'd brought and made up my mind to get to the bottom of this.

The moon was hidden in the clouds. Except for the bright light in my brother's room, everything was dark. Just as I was about to doze, some odd sounds suddenly came from Father's door. He walked toward it, as if he had noticed something. He stuck his head out a few times. The door was still half-open. I grew excited: sure enough, he was waiting for someone. It seemed I'd guessed right. Why did Father want to pour out his troubles to an outsider? Didn't he know that whatever he said would be exaggerated in ugly rumors? It was also possible that he wouldn't say anything bad about me to an outsider. Could it all be that third party's imagination? Normally, the family members (especially I) treated him quite well. You could say that, compared with most elderly people, he had nothing to complain of. Then who could this malevolent, backbiting guy be? My impression was that Father had never gone out, and that all of his friends and relatives had broken off relations with him years ago. I thought hard, yet I couldn't think of anyone who was still in contact with him. But Father had definitely met someone. It was this person who had spread gossip and slander among my colleagues.

I sat in the grove for a long time. Perhaps I fell asleep, or perhaps I dozed off from time to time. Anyhow, I didn't see anyone go to Father's room. The door was still half-open, letting out faint light from inside. After midnight, I saw Father walk to the door. He stood there talking with someone in the room as his broad back blocked the door. That person must have slipped in while I was dozing! I crept over to the window and kept close to the wall. Father's voice was rather hoarse. I could tell that he was quite excited.

". . . They're all only too anxious for me to die soon. When I say 'they,' of course that includes Rushu. She's still the main player. Whenever we eat, they're all acting. Rushu comes to see me on a set schedule. Why? She and I both know, and so I cut those things into pieces and destroyed them. This way, I'm leaving no traces behind. Who could really figure me out? Recent occurrences have alarmed all of them, especially Rushu. It absolutely never occurs to her that someday the corpse in the corner will come back to life. It doesn't occur to her, either, that some things that the outside world can never know will be exposed in this manner. The last two days, she has been distinctly haggard."

The person was talking with him in quite a low, hesitant voice, as if his nose were stopped up by a cold. I didn't get what he was saying, but he didn't pause. Sometimes, he even blubbered like a child. While the person talked, Father was smirking. His laughter was larded with the cough of the aged.

The plan I had originally worked out in the grove called for me to confront this person, but the situation caught me by surprise, because the malevolence didn't come from the outsider but from Father. I wasn't sure of that person's attitude, either. If I rushed in, I'd be on the horns of a dilemma. Father wasn't easy to deal with. Now I had definitely learned my lesson. Formerly, I had been so remiss and reckless.

Just then, Father walked from the door to the window, and he was talking just above my head, his voice both urgent and focused and evidently accompanied by gestures. When his words grew heated, he stamped his feet.

"While I'm still alive, I still have to do some things that I want to do. No one can stop me! I sit in this forgotten corner, thoughts thronging my mind. I've sat here year after year, year after year. Great changes have occurred in the outside world! They're busy with their own plans all day long. They all think I was done for long ago. Of course they can't imagine! Actually, this has been taking place for a long time. They're inwardly terrified. I know this just by looking at Rushu's face. It's so quiet at night: this is just about the best time . . ."

I stole back to my room. I wasn't brave enough to continue eavesdropping. At dawn, I was still thinking. Had that person left? Had he left? This midnight visitor: When and how on earth had he and Father gotten mixed up together? People are so hard to fathom!

———

Day after day passed, and at last the rumors gradually subsided. Although my colleagues still looked at me the same annoying way at work, I'd grown accustomed to it and so I wasn't as scared.

One day I was exhausted when I went home. As soon as I entered the door, my brother started in on the patriarchy thing again. He said that Father's position in the family jeopardized his life.

Whenever he braced himself to do something, he saw Father's face floating before him. So he became dejected and didn't want to do anything. This had been going on for a long time and he couldn't bear it. Sometimes he even thought he might as well do something really outrageous and then "run off without further ado."

Without the slightest hesitation, I said to him:

"Your absurd argument boggles my mind! That's total nonsense. Father stays in his room, and you guys never visit him: Isn't this the same as his not existing? Can't you at least overlook his existence? Sure, he eats with us every day, but he eats fast and he never sticks around long. And especially recently, he eats hardly anything. He just sits there going through the motions and then he leaves. How can he affect you so much? I think you're inwardly depressed and you can't do anything, so you want to extricate yourself and you blame others for this. But whom do you blame? An old man approaching death, the least important person in the family, a loner who has never meddled . . ."

"Hold on!" my brother interrupted me, and staring me in the face, he said, "Do you really think—do you really think that's what our father is like? You don't need to act so arrogant. I can't figure out what's going on between you, but at meals, I see your knees trembling."

"What have you heard?" I asked tensely.

"What could I have heard? None of this concerns me. The only reason for telling you what's on my mind is for our mutual benefit. Why can't you understand even this? Of course I don't intend to plot anything. What can I do? To be precise, all I'm doing is grumbling about the status quo." Moving closer, he whispered to me: "There were some suspicious sounds in his room just now."

I shrugged my shoulders and glanced at him scornfully. All of a sudden he blushed, and his eyes opened wide. Pointing straight ahead, he shouted: "Look! Look!"

At the end of the dim hallway, Father—wearing gray under-wear—was wobbling as he stood on a square stool. He was pounding a nail into the wall. His bare arm—only skin and bones—was extended from his unbuttoned sleeve, and he held a rusty hammer in his hand.

Faltering, Father got down from the stool and frowned as he said earnestly to me: "I want to hang a notebook here, or it could be called an account book, so that everyone will know where things stand. Rushu, you're good at keeping accounts, so of course you know: I've been retired all these years and have turned over all of my money to you and your siblings, but how much have I actually spent? You've noticed that I never go out. Except for food, I have no expenses, and recently I've eaten very little. Yet you tell me that you can barely make ends meet. Where has my money gone? These clothes—" With that, he pulled at the front of his undershirt. "These are my best clothes. All of you figure that since I don't go out, you don't need to make outerwear for me. This never even crosses your minds. The two jackets I have were both made by your grandma fifteen years ago when she was still alive!" He almost shouted this last sentence.

I was totally defeated. I was looking frantically in all directions. I was looking for my brother, but this slippery fellow had glided away without a trace. Father was holding the hammer high, as if preparing to fight.

"Papa! Papa! What are you saying?" Tears were mixed with my shouting.

"Rushu, help me hang that account book on this nail." His voice was composed and strong.

"No." I retreated a few steps and glared at him in desperation. "Father, don't force me. I can't do it."

"Okay. I'll do it myself."

He went back to his room and took the black notebook out of a cupboard. The book was fastened with fine hemp rope. As he entered his room, I noticed that all of the old books and letters had disappeared. The floor had been swept clean. Even the space under the bed was empty. When he walked out, he staggered again onto the square stool. The fine ropes on the book were tangled together, and it took him a long time to straighten them out and hang the notebook on a nail. While he was doing this, the stool kept swaying and creaking. I don't know why he hadn't steadied the stool before stepping onto it. His actions made me feel extremely tense, like an arrow held in a bowstring.

None of us knew what was recorded in the black notebook. We tacitly agreed that since Father had humiliated everyone in this despicable way, we'd better just ignore it. Would ignoring it put us at ease? I observed the four of them and found that didn't seem to be the case. They were fretful and uneasy. Every noon when Father was with us, he staggered up on the square stool, took the black notebook down, and carried it back to his room. One of us could never keep from saying: "Look, he's doing it again." The person seemed to be speaking scornfully, yet his hands were shaking. After a while, all of us looked down, and one by one we slipped out.

═══

One day I was asleep and having a long dream when Nishu knocked on my door. I looked at the clock: it was two in the morning. Nishu was pouting, and she was worriedly digging at her ear with her little finger. She hesitated a long time before saying:

"It was raining. I suddenly remembered the clothes hadn't been brought in from the courtyard, so I ran out there. I saw a light on in Father's room, and someone was standing in front of the window. It didn't appear to be Father because he was much taller than Father. Who was it? Someone had actually come calling on Father at midnight: Wasn't this frightening? The more I thought about it, the more uneasy I felt, so I ran into Father's room. The door was unlocked; it opened with a slight push. The strange thing was that Father was the only one in the room! Really. I peered into every corner. Maybe he had run into the hallway through that door. I didn't dare follow him into the hallway for fear that Father would get angry. In the incandescent light, Father's face was quite frightening. He kept laughing. I wasn't sure if he was angry or happy, so I retreated step by step all the way to the courtyard. By then the rain had stopped and the clothes were drenched so there was no point in bringing them in. I went back to my room. The more I thought about this, the more wrong I thought it was. So I came to find you. What do you think?"

After saying all of this in one breath, Nishu seemed very weary and couldn't keep her eyes open. She fell onto my bed in confusion and covered herself with my quilt. Soon, she was asleep. Nishu's news wasn't anything new, but after listening to her, I couldn't sleep. It wasn't a good idea to have the light on at midnight, so I turned it off and sat up in the dark. When I was half asleep, I seemed to hear the sound of something stirring in the hallway. As soon as I was more clear-headed, I realized that nothing was stirring. I was just hallucinating. That night, I opened the door twice and looked toward Father's room at the end of the hall. I noticed that his light was out. Not until daybreak did Nishu awaken. Rubbing her eyes, she said:

"The old shark had gone so far as to come out with that. I was arguing with him in my dream about that lost letter. Are you listening? I shouted until I was hoarse. Now my throat is burning."

Nishu used to call Father "shark" behind his back.

"From now on, you mustn't wander around at night. You overreacted when it was raining. It's no big deal if laundry gets wet. Just leave it."

"You're talking nonsense again." Laughing, she bent to tie her shoelaces. "I've tried not to meddle, but it didn't work. While I was in bed, I thought and thought. I thought of Father as an old spider in this house. His webs are everywhere. You run into them when you lift your head or stretch your hand out."

Then she finished lacing her shoes, leapt up, and ran out.

═══

I did my best to recall what day it was that Father had assumed control over the family. It seemed it had begun not long before, but it also seemed a long time ago. Maybe it had begun when I was in the cradle. The more I thought about it, the more blurred that boundary line became. In the end, I couldn't grasp it. On the surface, he had dropped out of life without our sensing it. Now it appeared that he had retreated in order to advance. I remembered going to his room one day when I had just become an adult, and saw him looking through a magnifying glass at traces of water at the foot of the wall. Arching his back, he was looking at it very earnestly.

"Rushu," he said to me, "This old wall has experienced everything. I always want to find some clues in it. This isn't asking too much, is it?"

"Of course—" I said hesitantly, "It doesn't matter."

"Good. Good girl. In times to come, you'll complain. You pay too much attention to minutiae. There's nothing I can hide from you."

At the time, his words sounded a little unreasonable. Only now as I recalled them did I understand. But did I really know what his purpose was? It was very likely that he was setting off a smoke bomb to distract me. So it made more sense to take it as a permanent rejection. This would put an end to useless illusions. He had said "There's nothing I can hide from you." Maybe this meant that he would hide everything from me. When he said "There's nothing I can hide from you," was it a way of ridiculing me? Or he might have had a longer-range plan and thus was scattering bait and waiting for the fish to take it? He had waited for so many years to pass: he was really patient. Now the fish had taken the bait and so he should feel gratified. But I noticed that in his excitement he grew thinner by the day. The gratification that he had fabricated for himself was poison to the nerves and gave him insomnia.

The other thing had occurred even earlier. I was about seven or eight at the time and had come back from playing outside when I heard him whispering with Grandmother. They were talking about a neighbor who had just died, and they were looking very serious.

"Rushu, if Grandma gets an infectious disease and the rest of you might catch it, what should be done?" Grandma asked.

I remember that she was reaching for me with her plump arms as she spoke in a kindly tone.

"Then we'd carry you out to the courtyard." I rolled my eyes and thought myself clever.

They both began laughing.

"Rushu is really bright." Father stood up excitedly and began pacing in the room.

Grandma's face brimmed with warm smiles. She patted me on my little head and let me go. I shot out of there like a bullet and quickly forgot the episode.

Now, remembering incidents from my childhood, I also recalled that Father and Grandma often chatted with each other. Was it beginning at that time, while they were chatting, that they masterminded my future? When I was a child, Grandma told me the story of the souls' night visits. Now, of course, I no longer believed those absurd tales, so who was the person Nishu saw?

I decided to ask Father directly.

When I went in, he was sitting with his eyes closed. In the shadows, his sunken cheeks made him look frightening.

"Who? Who else could it be?!" He said impatiently, "Of course it was I."

"Nishu—Shu said you aren't that tall." I stuttered.

"Damn! Can't I stand on a stool? Ah?" He glared as if he wanted to eat me.

"At work, I've heard a lot of rumors from my colleagues. I thought, if you really haven't gone out, how can others know what's going on here?"

"No wall can keep secrets inside."

He closed his eyes in exasperation, intending to ignore me.

——

I remember that in our childhood we always joked about Father behind his back. Laughing and joking, we made cynical remarks, as though none of us took him seriously.

One day, Father took me for a walk. He walked slowly with his hands behind his back, as if deep in thought. Back then, there weren't many cars, but only a few rickshaws. A thick layer of ash had accumulated on the blacktop road, and Father's old-fashioned leather shoes left footprints in the ash.

"Papa, why do you always wear these leather shoes? You don't even take them off at home. Didn't you ever wear any other shoes?"

Father's feet stopped in the ash, and he looked at me with a feeling of grief. I was frightened by my own joke. At a loss, I tugged at his clothes. He stopped for a long time—until someone came up from the opposite side of the street. Perhaps it was the person he'd been waiting for. It was a man of average height. His clothes were much like those that most drivers wore. His rough face was expressionless. He came over and shook hands with Father and referred to a promise the two of them had made earlier. Father replied, "I'm sorry! Sorry!" Disappointed, the other man walked away, swinging his arms. When he turned around, he glanced at me ominously. I shivered.

"Who was that?" I asked.

"He came to collect the debt that I owe him." With that, Father resumed walking in his old-fashioned shoes.

Following behind, I observed his footprints. Because he walked so gingerly, his footprints were always even. Not like mine—one footstep heavy, the next light: mine weren't at all uniform.

When we got home that day, a lot of guests were there. They were all Father's old friends who had come in a group to see him. Father was heavy-hearted as he entered the room. He waved at everyone and said, "The debt is due now."

The guests seemed uneasy about him. With one voice, they said: "Isn't there any room for delay?"

"Unfortunately no."

Dispirited, Father lowered his head. His expression was anguished. The guests gestured to one another and quietly left.

After they left, Father raised his head and looked at me in a swivet and said, "Rushu, in fact, the debt doesn't have to be paid now. I can keep putting it off. You can repay it for me in the future, okay?"

Afraid, I retreated to the door. I didn't know if I was afraid of really assuming the debt or if I was afraid that I didn't grasp what he meant. Actually, I didn't understand what he'd said at all, and I was all the more afraid because I didn't understand. I held on to the door, preparing to run off.

"I was kidding you. Don't you want to help Papa at all?"

"No," I blurted out.

"Okay. That's good. I feel reassured." He looked as if he'd suddenly seen the light.

Father died in the harsh winter. His large body was bent into a curved bow. One hand turned into a firm fist placed on his chest. I stood at the head of his bed, my inner curiosity rising little by little: What was he holding in his hand? The people from the funeral home hadn't arrived yet, and the other family members were outside preparing for the service. Taking advantage of their absence, I hurriedly knelt in front of the bed and seized Father's cold fist and tried my best to open it. I tried for a long time, but it wouldn't open. I felt Father moving. I sat down on the floor and trembled. From behind, I heard someone say coldly: "Truly diabolical."

I looked around: my brother was standing at the door.

"Who are you talking about?"

"You, of course! You scared him to death! And even now you won't let go of him! Ah, I saw through your plan a long time ago. Why didn't I stop you? It's only because of my selfishness! Sometimes, I'm weak, but I've never hurt anyone. Ah, Father! Father! This was all her scheme . . ." Choked with sobs, he was having hysterical spasms.

All the family members assembled, and my brother was carried out. Nishu quietly squatted down with me.

"That night, I shouldn't have gone to your room and talked about Father." She said, "I was always estranged from him—not like the relationship between the two of you, with so many personal feelings. It was because I was having insomnia and the rain was really irritating that I wanted to talk with you. So I just made up an excuse to see you. Actually, I hadn't seen anything and even if I had, I wouldn't have gossiped . . ."

"Get out!!" I roared.

She stood up at once and left.

Had Father really moved? Of course not. It was just my imagination. His body seemed coiled up even tighter.

Outside, firecrackers sounded, along with shouts and the sound of talking. Father's friends from long ago had arrived. They had responded very quickly, just like flies that smelled spoiled meat. I hadn't run into them on the street for years; they were mysterious guys. Ordinarily, they were nowhere to be seen, but in a crisis they all rushed out together. All of a sudden, I felt really afraid. I looked out the window and saw my brother leading them into the courtyard. I wanted to find a place to hide. Why did I alone have to take on Father's debt? During his lifetime, he had never briefed me about these debts. After all, I can always walk away. I can leave and go to the unpeopled borderland.

It's the 28th today, and my owner has run out of patience. Ever since breakfast he's been looking out the window. I can hear all his pores growling, and his eyes are flashing a fluorescent green. He's a cultured man, a bachelor with time on his hands. A person like him doesn't usually show his brutality unless he's really provoked. At breakfast, he kicked me on the forehead and I fainted at once. What led to this? Milk. That's right—milk. Naturally, he knows how much I love milk: previously, he had always split a bottle of milk with me. But this morning, because of the black person, everything went wrong. Without paying any attention to me, my owner had poured the whole bottle of milk into his bowl. I'd lost no time in tugging at his pant-leg, and had also called him softly, but he had ignored me. It seemed he was going to drink it all, so in my anxiety, I nipped his leg—not a real bite, just a reminder. Who'd have guessed that he would explode? Later, I figured this had given him an excuse to do what he'd been wanting to do anyway. Definitely! If a person was nursing grudges, then he'd stop at nothing. When I came to not long afterward, I realized that I'd better reassess my relationship with him. Delving into it more deeply, I concluded there was nothing superficial about it. Maybe the word "ownership" not only connoted dependency and obedience, but also, at some point, conflict and manipulation. After all, I knew the secret relationship between him and the black man, didn't I?

In fact, my owner had no reason to lose his patience, for I knew that sooner or later, the black man would pay another visit to this small high-rise apartment. It was three o'clock in the morning a year ago when my owner got out of bed and went to the kitchen in search of something to eat. I noticed he was barefoot, not even wearing slippers. When he walked, he held his arms out in front of him, and his face was blank. I knew he was walking in his sleep. Since he'd done this several times without ever having a problem, I didn't tag along. He opened the refrigerator, took out a beer and some cold cuts, and sat at the tea table to enjoy them. Smacking his lips, he ate with great relish, but I knew he wasn't awake. Perhaps food tasted even better in dreams than in reality. I was itching to go over and mooch some. But I didn't. I couldn't wake him up at such a time; that would have been harmful to his health.

Just then, someone rapped on the door three times. Who could it be in the dead of night? My sleepwalking owner heard it at once and got up and opened the door. I thought, if it's a thief, he's a goner for sure: with one blow, a thief would make sure he'd never wake up again. Luckily, it wasn't a thief, but a man with lacquer-black skin. He was wearing a shiny gold chaplet around his neck, and two skull-shaped silver rings on his fingers. My owner nodded at him and said, "It's you." The fellow answered laconically, "Yes." I could see that my owner wasn't awake yet—he was moving stiffly. After the fellow sat down, my owner brought him some food from the refrigerator, and soon the tea table was loaded down with all kinds of cold cuts, sausages, and thousand-year-old eggs. The black man sat up straight and clenched his teeth, unwilling to loosen up at all. He didn't touch the snacks, but denounced my owner with his eyes. My owner didn't notice; perhaps he was "seeing without seeing"—as sleepwalkers generally do.

"Won't you have a little beer?" my owner asked.

"My chest hurts." As he talked, the black man tore his shirt open with a single motion. "I was burned in the forest fire . . ."

There wasn't a hair on his bare black chest. You could see the distinct throbbing on the lower left side of his chest: Was something wrong with his heart?

My owner didn't look up at him. He was muttering to himself, "Why won't he even drink beer?"

The black man was grinding his teeth—to me, this sounded like a duck quacking—and rubbing his feet surreptitiously on the floor. In order to relieve the tension, I sprang to his lap and deployed some feminine charms. The black man petted me with his beringed hand, but it wasn't ordinary petting, for his fingers were gripping my throat harder and harder. I began struggling, clawing the air aimlessly. When I was just on the edge of losing consciousness, he pushed me down to the floor. I was afraid he would hurt me again, so I played dead. At the time, my owner seemed unaware of what was going on. I saw him pacing restlessly back and forth in the room, maybe waiting for the black man to start something. As for me, since I'd already been the target of the black man's malice, I was afraid he would do something even worse.

As the black man stood up to leave, my owner humbly begged him to stay a while longer.

"My chest hurts. Your room is suffocating," he said as he flung the door open.

He left. My owner—his sleepwalker's arms held out in front of him—seemed about to follow him, but instead, he just walked absently around the room, repeating over and over again, "Why couldn't I get him to stay? Why couldn't I get . . ."

═══

My owner was a serious stuffed-shirt of a man. He had a job at a newspaper office, but as a rule he worked at home. I had settled down here quite by accident. At the time, my former owner had taken his anger out on me and thrown me out. With nowhere to go, I'd been loafing around on the stairs when, all of a sudden, I saw a door open a crack. A thread of light came out. In the wee hours of the pitch-black night, the thread of light stared at me and cheerily beckoned me inside. The room was clean, with everything in its place. My present owner was sitting on the sofa, deep in thought, one hairy arm propped up on the armrest, his huge head in his hands. He saw me at once and jumped up and said, "Ha! An old cat!" From then on, my name was "Old Cat."

I quickly realized I was more comfortable here than with my former owner. My starchy new owner was not the least bit stiff with me: trusting me to discipline myself, he never set limits for me. After thoroughly inspecting his domicile, I, a cat of some breeding, chose the rug beneath the tea table as my bedroom.

Every day, I dined with my owner. Since he believed in equal rights, we each had our own bowls and saucers. I ate whatever he ate, except that I didn't drink beer, nor did I like fruit.

My owner was efficient in his work. As a rule, he worked for two hours in the middle of the night, and then sat around the whole day, as if afflicted by a certain kind of depression. I sympathized with him: I supposed he was unhappy with his life or frustrated in his work. I also thought that he was essentially a strong person, and that after getting over the present difficulty, he'd be fine. But I'd been here a long time now, and not only had he not improved, but his depression was even worse than before. Had he been unhappy all along? After some consideration, I rejected this view. One day, a wretched-looking person came over. He meekly called my owner "editor-in-chief," thus making it clear that he was a colleague from the newspaper office: from this, I concluded that everything was going well at work. I also discovered that, for no reason, my owner looked for trouble. Except for the two hours that he shut himself up in his bedroom and worked—I had no way of knowing what he was like then—most of the rest of the time he was an unhappy man.

One day, he asked someone to hang an iron pothook from the living room ceiling, and from it he hung a hemp rope. When I came back from a stroll, the door was open, and as soon as I went in, I saw him dangling, unmoving, from that hemp rope. I screamed in terror, and he began swaying. He stood on tiptoe on the table, loosened the noose, and jumped down. The rope left two purple marks on his neck. After freeing himself from the noose, he looked much more relaxed and was actually in high spirits as he went to the kitchen and fried an ocean fish for me. But it was hard for him to get into such a good mood. As I ate, I was watching him in terror and thought to myself, is this a vale-dictory dinner? Of course it wasn't, because after a bath, he strode briskly into his bedroom to work. The next day, his old trouble recurred: now, besides being depressed, he was also in agony. His intermittent roaring was oppressive.

In order to help him, I jumped up and nipped his hand. This little trick worked: he calmed down as if just waking from a dream, and he urged me to bite him a little harder, until I drew blood. My owner must have been possessed by a demon, making it impossible for him to focus his energy on anything at all the whole day long. He couldn't find any way, either, to vent his unhappiness. Or perhaps he had too high an opinion of himself to try any of the ordinary ways of venting. Sometimes, self-abuse could temporarily postpone the ultimate destruction, but it couldn't solve the root problem. Each time, it took more intense stimulation. Just when all of his remedies were almost exhausted, the weird black man had appeared, thus instantly changing his entire attitude toward life.

That night, after the black man left, my owner slept for a long time. He didn't wake up until the third morning, forgetting even his work responsibilities. After he woke up, he pulled out of his depression and rushed to the balcony, where he lifted weights over and over. Then he began sweeping the apartment. He cleaned the place until it was spotless, and even went so far as to buy a flower to brighten the living room. He washed the heavy drapes and let the sunshine splash the living room: the whole room overflowed with the atmosphere of spring. I really didn't like his turning everything upside down in the apartment: the dust he stirred up made it impossible for me to breathe, and the rose made me sneeze uncontrollably. My owner wasn't young. How could he be so hyperactive? He was acting almost like a teenager. The only thing I could do to get away from his cleaning was to go out and stand on the stairs.

He kept this up for a long time. His face reddened and his eyes flashed. But every morning, and again at dusk, he looked bewildered, expectant. At such times, he strolled to the balcony and fixed his eyes on the distant sky. I knew who he was waiting for, but I couldn't help him. Despite my anxiety, I was unable to do anything.

The black man was savage and cruel. I'd already experienced his strong grip, and I didn't know why he had eventually left me with my life. My owner was good to me, but as soon as this black man arrived, he simply didn't give me another thought. He was indifferent to the black man's brutal treatment of me. I felt vaguely hurt. My owner thought constantly about the one rogue whom he'd encountered while dreaming, even to the point of making him the center of his life. This made me quite angry. Wasn't I the one who kept him company day and night? Wasn't I his only companion during his lonely days? When he was in the depths of despair, when all the fun had gone out of his life, who jumped on his lap and comforted him? But then, thinking about it more dispassionately, perhaps my affection had always been unrequited. My owner was an extraordinary man—unfathomable and mulling everything over at length. Even a particularly sensitive cat like me couldn't catch anything but the surface of his ideas. Now, since he was looking forward to the black man coming, he must have had his own reasons. I'd better not impose my views on him. In a few minutes that night, my sleepwalking owner must have communicated at the speed of lightning with the black man. This kind of communication was far beyond my comprehension.

With a charcoal pencil, my owner drew a pair of eyes and hung them on the living room wall. At a glance, I knew whose eyes they were. That man's penetrating stare had left a deep impression on me. When my owner finished his work in the middle of the night and emerged from his inner sanctum, he looked exhausted and he would sometimes stand beneath that drawing and mumble something for a while. I thought, my owner was waiting for his idol: all he could do was console himself with false hopes and meet with him that way. The black man's mysterious comings and goings were hard on him. Judging from his behavior that night, the black man also felt unbearable agony. It made him sort of unearthly. What I mean is: his suffering had gone beyond this world. This was different from my owner's suffering. I felt that, although my owner was unconventional, his anguish stemmed from everything he did. Although I was a cat, able to observe dispassionately, I really didn't know whether this black man had anything to do with this world. When he gripped my throat with both hands, he did so unconsciously. That's to say, he didn't know that it was my throat he had gripped. Why did my owner feel so attracted to this sort of fellow?

After the first rush passed, my owner was no longer so overstimulated: he entered into a period of calm. Every day, he hid out in his inner sanctum and worked for two hours. Then he frittered away the rest of the time. Aside from making purchases and occasionally going to the newspaper office, he didn't go out. During this period, a clerk from the office came by once. He was an old man with a thin, sallow face, who had come to bring drafts. He left a bad impression on me, probably because of the thumbtack in the sole of his shoe. After he came in, he scuffed the gleaming floor, leaving a lot of metallic marks on it. This man wasn't clean, either; he smelled sour, and he spat wherever he pleased. My ever-starchy owner, however, didn't seem to mind any of this: he led the clerk warmly over to the sofa, seated him, and poured a beer for him. They evidently had a special relationship.

"Has he been to the newspaper office?" My owner seemed fearful as he asked this.

"I asked the receptionist. I was told that he just stood in the lobby for three minutes and then left." The old man sipped his beer calmly, his eyes flashing maliciously: he was obviously taking pleasure in my owner's misfortune.

"Are you sure he said three minutes?"

"That's exactly right."

My owner slumped onto the sofa: a load had been lifted from his shoulders.

The old clerk had left some time ago, but my owner was still agitated by the news he had brought. I couldn't figure out whether my owner was happy that the black man had gone to his workplace or whether he was fearful. My owner was so jumpy that he couldn't sit still, couldn't eat much, and couldn't sleep. I noticed that he was dazed as he sat on the sofa. He sat there for two hours, often simpering, as if he'd picked up something valuable. While he was in this trance, disaster befell me: he completely overlooked my existence. Sometimes I was hungry and thirsty and jumped onto his lap and kept meowing, but my entreaties didn't move him at all! In desperation, I tried to open the refrigerator myself, but I couldn't. Finally, thank God, he thought of food. My stomach was grumbling, and my paws kept quivering. I snagged a sausage from his hand and ate it, but I wanted another and there weren't any more. He was preoccupied with eating, and didn't even hear my cries. My owner's behavior infuriated me: after all, I was a living thing, not an ornament. I had to eat, drink, shit, and piss every day, just as he did. In his care, I had long since become aware of my equal rights. I had to make him notice this! I decided to start championing my rights. When my owner opened the refrigerator, I scurried in: I wanted to eat to my heart's content!

He didn't see me, and he closed the refrigerator door on me. I found the fried ocean fish that he'd been saving and wolfed it down right away. While I was eating, I felt more and more that something was wrong. The frightening chill not only coursed through my hair, but also pierced my guts. It quickly became difficult for me to take even a tiny step. Crouching on the refrigerator shelf, I soon lost consciousness. I had a long, troubling dream, in which the sky was filled with frost-shaped butterflies. Two of them fluttered and landed on the tip of my nose. After moistening my hot breath, they melted into two streams that ran down my face: I couldn't stop sneezing.

This nap came close to killing me. When I woke up, I was lying on the rug in my owner's bedroom. It was the first time I'd been to his bedroom, for I had always considered it his inner sanctum. The furnishings were so simple that they lent the room an air of poverty: a hard wooden bed, wooden chairs, a rough desk, and a bookshelf heaped with documents. This room used to have windows, but my owner had hammered them shut with plywood: not a thread of light could get in. On the right-hand wall was a weak fluorescent light—the only source of light in the room. I wanted to cry out, but my frozen mouth and throat hadn't recovered yet. I couldn't move, either.

"Why do you have to learn my ways? A few days ago, I hanged

myself at home: this was psychologically necessary. It's only because I'm a person that I have these peculiar needs. You're a cat: even if you understood me better, you couldn't become a human. So you can't possibly have the kind of psychological needs that I have. Isn't that right? Now look at the state you're in. I feel terribly guilty. You shouldn't have gone into the refrigerator. You don't belong there. If you're so hungry, you can always take a bite out of my leg. Why didn't you do that? You're too soft, and that isn't good for either of us. It will just make me even more treacherous. Even more cold-blooded. Can you hear me? If you can, move your eyeballs, please!'"

I had never thought of my owner as an ugly person, but after he finished talking to himself, I thought he was extremely ugly. Yet, he talked so reasonably! He'd been at his desk, with his back to me, when he said these things. He wouldn't see me move my eyeballs, even if I did. I made an effort to open my eyes, but he had slumped into deep thought. I heard someone going up and down the stairs. Was it he?!

———

After the refrigerator incident, I had a bum leg and now I limped inelegantly. Overcome by remorse, my owner raised my standard of living. I had fresh fish and milk at almost every meal. And because I ate too much and exercised too little, I frequently had diarrhea. My injury left a big impression on my owner. He was worrying about me more and more, so he had to change his ways. Every morning, he had to go to the market and buy food—and not just for himself. His main concern now was giving me three meals a day. Now and then, he also added some delicacies to my diet—things like seaweed and dried fish. He was gradually beginning to live like an ordinary person. Inwardly, I had conflicting reactions to this. Although I was secretly happy, I also felt guilty and a little uneasy. I felt that my owner was making sacrifices for me, and that this could lead to unfortunate consequences. For sure, he wasn't an ordinary person, but one with special requirements. Now, he was reining in his very nature: Could this lead to an outbreak of its dark side? You have to know that, before I came into his life, he had lived for decades without caring about anything, and he had never compromised himself for anything, either.

But, gradually, it became apparent that I was worrying too much. My injury hadn't made my owner any more abnormal. Quite the opposite: he perked up a little. He had a lot more to do and was no longer as idle as he used to be. If people were a little particular about their daily lives, fixing three meals a day and cleaning the apartment could take up a lot of time. When I was first hurt, my owner was still not enamored of doing these things, because he'd long been accustomed to a simple life. At that time, everything in the refrigerator was prepared food, but now he had to buy fresh food and he had to cook especially for me. So sometimes he was almost scurrying about. Since he was very capable, he quickly had the housework under control. Recently, he even seems quite enthusiastic about doing the housework, for he whistles as he works! As it is now, he doesn't have much time for woolgathering—except after he gets up in the morning, when he can't help but sink into daydreams for a short time. Then, as if he's heard an alarm, he springs up and "plunges into the flood of daily work" (this is the sentence I use to describe him).

Something occurred that surprised me a lot. One day, when I returned from a stroll, I saw the black man standing at our door. He seemed irresolute, but then he went in. Five seconds later, he came out again. He looked the same: teeth clenched, eyes menacing. Like a thick black shadow, he dodged into the elevator and quietly descended. When I went inside, my owner was wearing an apron and busying himself with cooking fish soup. What had transpired in those five seconds? Had they had a brief talk, or had my owner not even seen this uninvited guest for whom he lived day and night? After looking into it, I decided the latter was the most likely. Could it be that the idol in his heart was collapsing?

The next day, I looked at him even more carefully. I stared at him early in the morning when he was daydreaming on the balcony. My observation told me that what he hoped for from the bottom of his heart hadn't faded at all, but was even more intense because of the telescoped time. Gripping the railing convulsively, he was looking at the horizon: I was afraid he would jump from this high building. After a while, tears of regret filled his eyes. What did he regret? Had he been unaware of the black man's presence and then learned of it later from traces that had been left behind? Then why had he grown so numb that he even missed the arrival of the person whom he yearned for day and night? As I saw it, although the black man moved as if floating on water, he couldn't be completely soundless. I could only conclude that everyday life had numbed my owner's senses. By the time I thought of this, he had already calmed down. He rinsed his feverish face with cold water. Then, without looking back, he picked up his shopping basket and went to the market. He had a lot more self-control now.

He must have been working much more efficiently. Sometimes I saw him go into his inner sanctum and re-emerge within the hour. And in his work he seemed even more flushed with success. He still wasn't close to anyone: he was sticking to his lonely bachelor's existence. It was from the old clerk's mouth that I learned of my owner's promotion: I heard the old man call him "big boss." He also reproached him for living so simply, and said he should try to have some fun. At the time, I had a sudden thought—if the black man told him to give up everything and go with him to the ends of the earth, would he do it? What followed proved me absolutely wrong.

As a rule, my owner went to the office only once every two weeks, because another big boss was in charge of the day-to-day work. My owner frequently discussed work with him on the phone. Sometimes someone from the office also telephoned, but not very often. Recently, all of this had changed a lot: now our phone rang all the time. From my observations, in general, these people weren't calling him about work, but were complaining about some old scores that hadn't been evened up. These people evidently belonged to all kinds of opposing factions. They were all attacking each other. My owner's responses seemed very odd—he showered compliments on everyone who called, and parroted what they said, so on the phone everyone was happy. As a spectator, I heard a lot of conflicting words coming out of his mouth. Today he said this, the next day he said that: he was glib on the phone, but after hanging up, he kept sighing and was endlessly remorseful, absolutely fed up. Still, the next time the phone rang, he rushed to answer it again. Sometimes this meant he had to put off doing the housework. I was very much repulsed by those "gossips" from the newspaper office. I thought they were all vermin. At the same time, I was captivated: How could an aloof, idiosyncratic character like my owner care about his despicable underlings, even going so far as to mingle with them in the cesspool? To show my revulsion, I jumped on the tea table several times and pretended it was an accident when I knocked the phone off the hook so that there couldn't be any incoming calls. But my owner had recently become especially vigilant. Every once in a while he checked to see whether the phone was back on the hook. It was as if he had eyes in the back of his head, so my little plot failed.

Things grew more and more serious. Phone calls weren't enough for those people: I heard them pressuring my owner to deal with their disputes. It seemed that everyone who called asked my owner to "give evidence" on his behalf. I secretly felt things were going from bad to worse. I grumbled to myself that my owner was too unprincipled: he shouldn't mingle with those people and intervene in their filthy mess. After each phone call he was terribly distressed, and didn't get over it for a long time. After a few more days, these people began to press their demands even more forcefully, and there were even a few menacing implications. One of them mentioned the black man: he said the black man had presented himself at the newspaper office's lobby and was waiting for my owner to meet him there. After my owner took this phone call, he paled and grew weak in the knees. In a daze, he tidied up a little and then rushed to the newspaper office. The rest of the day, I felt as if I had dropped into hell. I believed that his going there this time boded ill—that a collective plot to murder him was going to be actualized.

It was late at night before he returned. Not only had he not lost his life, but he was in such high spirits that he was singing in the bathroom. After a bath, he was full of energy as he went into his inner sanctum to work.

The next day, the phone was ringing off the hook again: my owner kept using vulgar language on the phone and telling dirty jokes. He seemed a changed man, but except for the phone calls, he was still treating me well. He found time for housework and seemed in good spirits. I thought I'd better get used to his new ways. I should make an effort to observe his train of thought and catch up with it. In the afternoon, the black man asked someone to phone and tell him to go to the office (I figured this out from my owner's expression). When he heard this, he took off immediately, beside himself with agitation. After these two times, I finally got it: it was the black man's idea that my owner should mingle with the others in the cesspool!

That evening, he brought two ugly guys back with him. Each one sat on the sofa, crossed his legs, chain-smoked, and spat on the floor. Before they'd been here even a minute, they began talking about the old clerk, hinting that he was a sycophant. I knew that my owner and the clerk were on very good terms, and that they agreed about everything in their work. I couldn't understand why he was letting these people slander him. He sat there listening gravely and nodding his head slightly, indicating that he sided with them. Thus encouraged, the older one was emboldened to suggest that my owner tell the old clerk "to get another line of work" and give his position to someone else. As the old guy was talking, the door creaked and opened: the black man was standing there. In the light from the corridor, his face looked ashen and was etched with deep grief. Pea-sized beads of perspiration rolled down from his forehead. He was shaking badly. The old guy stopped talking, and everyone stared at the black man outside the door. Suddenly, it was as if the black man had been shot in the neck: all at once, his head drooped. An invisible force was dragging him back, all the way to the elevator door. As soon as the door opened, he tumbled into the elevator, and it slid swiftly down.

"He's a guy who really means well and always has to be in the thick of things, even if they're none of his business." The ugly old guy sighed, "If he knew that someone as dishonest as the old clerk was mixed up with us, he'd want you to get rid of him, too. What do you say?"

"I guess you're right. I guess so."

My owner was agreeing absent-mindedly, but he was still staring at the elevator, as though the black man would suddenly step out of it. I was not pleased with my owner's behavior. It had never crossed my mind that he could change so much. Sometimes he looked almost like a "scoundrel." But why on earth was the black man grieving so deeply? It also occurred to me that since my owner was able to get along with people now, perhaps he no longer needed me. I had always thought he did. When I was alone with him, it was the two of us against the world. I reveled in this. Now that this defiance was gone, would he kick me out? After all, he'd agreed to get rid of the old clerk, hadn't he? The more I thought about this, the more I despaired. If he kicked me out, all I could do was hang out on the stairs, because I couldn't be so heartless as to abandon him. Someday, he would need me.

I was most repelled by the younger visitor. He didn't talk, but he was constantly drumming his feet, jiggling the table so much that the soft drinks fell to the floor and made a mess of the rug. You have to remember that this rug was my bed. I really wanted to bite his leg, but this guy was as agile as an acrobat. And so I not only didn't succeed in biting him, but I also landed on the floor, unable to move, when he kicked me in the back.

My owner said, "My cat always has to get the best of others."

This infuriated me.

My owner was probably afraid the guy would hurt me again, so he carried me to his bedroom, put me on the wooden bed, and then closed the door. I fell asleep and didn't even know when those people left.

I woke up at midnight and saw my owner scribbling excitedly at the table, his inspiration gushing like a spring. From behind, he looked like a lunatic. I didn't understand the things he wrote—newspapers were out of my element—but I did know that this time my owner had climbed to a very high plane and was more exhilarated than other people could ever be. I was happy for him. You have to remember that only a few hours earlier I was worried that he had become a "scoundrel." His rapid change was beyond my comprehension.

Seeing that I was awake, he walked over and sat next to me, sighing as he talked.

"Old Cat, why did you have to offend my colleagues? You really should stop being so self-righteous. See, you learned a painful lesson this time. I also know that you purposely took the phone off the hook so that my colleagues couldn't get through. Why did you bother? You must realize that even if they can't get through on the phone, they can think of other ways to get in touch with me. No one can keep them away. Even though you're one smart cat, you'd better understand that my thoughts are a lot more profound than yours. For example, these colleagues of mine: you think they're too vulgar for words, and so you scorn them. I don't see it that way. They truly care about me; otherwise, they wouldn't come so far to see me. You mustn't be hostile toward them; you should think of them as friends. That would be a big help to me. Old Cat, you have to believe me. If even you don't believe me, what meaning would my life have?"

By the end, he was talking quite tearfully. Although I didn't appreciate his words one bit, his affection moved me. So I also cried. Both of us wept.

After I had cried for a while, my back also felt much better. I had no reason not to believe my owner. No matter what kind of person he was, I had to believe him, come hell or high water. I made up my mind: even if he sometimes got fed up with being a person of integrity and wanted to be a "scoundrel," I would still be loyal to him. As he said, he was much more profound than I was, so I'd better not judge his behavior on the basis of superficial things.

After I had thought this through, my back pain vanished. I stood up, climbed onto his lap, and snuggled at his chest. The two of us wept silently again. I wasn't too sure why I was crying. Was I touched? Was it a mix of sadness and happiness? Or was it a certain regret? Or a certain sympathy? My owner's tears must have meant something even more complex. Since I couldn't figure it out, I would just muddle along and stick with him. My owner, who had been so excited in the daytime, was now shedding so many tears that my hair was all wet. He kept repeating in a hoarse voice, "Ai, Old Cat—ai, Old Cat . . ."

After this, we went to the kitchen for a great meal of sausage, smoked fish, and milk. While we were eating this wonderful midnight repast, I suddenly felt much closer to my owner. As he had in the past, he raised a glass of beer, and then his hand stopped for a couple of seconds in midair before he finally brought the glass slowly to his lips. He didn't drink the beer in one gulp, but sipped a mouthful and held it in his mouth, shilly-shallying for a long time before swallowing it. I had long been used to this habit of his, and hadn't paid much attention to it, but tonight I felt there was something new about it. As I stared at him, I realized that he needed me to understand him thoroughly.

My owner grew uneasy under my gaze. Setting his glass down, he asked, "Does anyone in this world feel an affection that's deeper than our affection for each other?"

Even so, when all is said and done, I didn't completely understand him. Perhaps the only thing I could do was wait patiently, wait until everything cleared up of its own accord, wait until the black man who came and went without a trace met up with him again, and divulged even more about the mystery of life.

The compound where Uncle Lou lives has a pleasant name—"Village in the Big City." Because the power was off that day, I climbed twenty-four flights of stairs to reach his small loft on the top floor. As I stood at the entrance, I was dimly aware that the old pain in my foot was coming back. Damn! Why did I have to seek out Uncle Lou right now? Because I could no longer bear the inner panic. This is what was happening: for several days, as soon as I woke up, I felt strange because I couldn't touch my face. I stretched my hand out toward the place where my face was supposed to be, but I could touch only my hair. And my hair was coarser than usual: it even pricked my hand. After a while, when I looked in a small mirror, my face returned to normal. Then, in the interval before I looked in the mirror, what was my face like? I put the small mirror back under the pillow, so that as soon as I opened my eyes in the morning, I could look in the mirror. It was strange, for when I looked in the mirror, nothing was there but the bed's headboard. I touched my face again, but I could still touch only my coarse hair. There were also some grain-shaped things on my scalp, like the coarse sand that adheres to sandpaper. I put away the mirror and waited a while to look again. This time, I saw my face, and there was certainly nothing abnormal about it.

Uncle Lou had been my next-door neighbor when we both lived in an old house. We hadn't seen each other for a long time, so—standing at his door now—I hesitated a little.

It was strange: the door wasn't closed, and yet, though I knocked several times, no one answered. After pushing the door and entering, I saw Uncle Lou sitting upright in front of the window and looking into the distance. Even after all these years, Uncle Lou didn't seem to be getting a bit older; although he was more than seventy, his hair was still black. The room was neat and clean, the furniture simple—a bed, a chest of drawers, a dining table, and a few chairs. That was all. The kitchen was in a corner under the slanted ceiling. There was a window, so Uncle Lou could look at the cityscape as he cooked. A few shallots were on the stove, and next to the stove stood a small bamboo basket of eggs. The old man was leading a decent life. This was a relatively large loft, with several windows on the south, north, and east sides. Living here was like living in a glass greenhouse. With the sun high in the sky, it was uncomfortably hot in the room, yet Uncle Lou was relaxed and calm. I really admired him.

"Are you observing our city, Uncle Lou?"

"No, I'm waiting for someone."

That was weird. He'd known I was coming. Perhaps, sitting at the window, he'd seen me enter this residential area. If I wasn't the one he was waiting for, who was it? It was no secret that he'd been trying to stay away from others for a long time. For example, he was the one who had taken the initiative more than ten years earlier to hold me at arm's length. And yet now, he was waiting for someone! It really wasn't the right time for me to have come. Should I leave?

"Uncle Lou, I'm leaving. I'll come back another time."

"No, Hedgehog, why not wait with me? The sun is so nice."

I was shocked, because Hedgehog was my deceased younger brother. I had stood here so long, and he hadn't looked at me even once. Following Uncle Lou's line of vision, I looked out and saw a water tower in the distance, as well as the post office, the tax office, various other large buildings, and the mirage-obscured suburban quarry. I blinked, and it suddenly changed into a vast expanse of whiteness. I looked hard again, but it was still the vast expanse of whiteness. And thus, the anxiety I had experienced this morning rose again from the bottom of my heart.

"Uncle Lou, I'm not Hedgehog. I'm Puppy. I'm Puppy—the one who used to go fishing in the creek with you. Sure, I've degenerated a lot over the years . . ." I was starting to babble.

"Puppy? Aren't Puppy and Hedgehog the same person?"

Uncle Lou still hadn't looked at me even once. What was he looking at? I was distressed because I couldn't see anything. Feeling as if my knee had been gnawed by a little animal, I sat down on a chair. At last, Uncle Lou faced me, and only then did I get a good look at his face. His brown face not only wasn't getting any older, it looked even younger than in the past. The wrinkles that had previously lined his forehead had fled. But one thing bothered me: his gaze was flickering. In the past, his gaze had always been focused.

"He's arrived," Uncle Lou said, and with that, he appeared to be really satisfied.

"Who is he?"

Uncle Lou didn't reply, but only listened attentively. I did, too, and heard footsteps that sounded odd: the sound neither came closer nor did it recede. That is to say, he was neither coming up the stairs nor going down. He went up and down between the twenty-third and twenty-fourth floors. I listened for a while, and then the sound stopped. I wanted to get up and look out the door, but the stabbing sensation in my knee hurt so much that I broke into a cold sweat. Uncle Lou asked:

"Have you remembered?"

I didn't know what he meant. I couldn't speak. I was sweating all over.

All of a sudden, Uncle Lou clambered up to the windowsill and sat there with one leg swinging back and forth in midair.

"If you clench your teeth hard, you'll feel no pain. In the past, a lot of crocodiles bit my legs in the lake. When I clenched my teeth, they swam away. This room of mine is linked with the lake. Have you remembered?"

Sure enough, when I clenched my teeth, the pain eased. In this "lake," this loft from which you looked out and saw nothing clearly, what did I recall? I recalled the playing cards I had lost as a child. It was a deck of expensive waxed playing cards that I cared about very much. Four people had been in the room that afternoon. Who had stolen the cards? This was a frightening question. And what's more, a storm that afternoon caused a flood that ruined our floor boards. For a short time, the city was a vast expanse of whiteness. Was it rainwater or lake water?

"I think you've remembered a little something, haven't you?"

Uncle Lou jumped down happily from the windowsill. He was as agile as a thirty-year-old. I replied that I had remembered one incident, but that I didn't understand the point of his question. It was even hotter in the room, probably because the sun was higher. Uncle Lou walked quietly to the door and looked out. Then he walked back and said to me, "That person has gone down." He also said that he was anxious every day, because he waited for him every day. He sometimes came and sometimes didn't; he was absolutely inconsistent. "He's my nephew from the countryside."

I was looking at the large window on the south side. I saw the sun, which was like a circle made of metal flakes—a white circle without dazzling rays, a solitary circle hanging in the boundless sky. Then, could it be that the dry heat in this room wasn't coming from the sun? I wiped the sweat from my face with my sleeve. I wanted to stand up, but my feet couldn't manage it. I looked at Uncle Lou again. He said he passed his life feeling "anxious," but he didn't feel at all hot in this sauna. He wasn't sweating; he looked fresh and energetic.

"Uncle Lou, why didn't this relative of yours come inside?"

"He can't. He's too ugly."

"What? I never heard of such a thing!"

Uncle Lou sat down on the windowsill again. This time, both legs were swinging in midair. This frightened me a little, but he was relaxed, as though there were lake water outside the window and he could swim across it.

I could still hear footsteps on the stairs, so I thought the ugly relative hadn't left yet. Why did Uncle Lou wait every day for this relative who was so ugly that he couldn't associate with others? And since he was too ugly to be with others, then why did Uncle Lou insist that I wait with him in the room? Alas, Uncle Lou: in the more than ten years since I'd seen him, he'd become an enigma of an old man.

After wiping my face with the washcloth he handed me, I became a little more clear-headed. Clenching my teeth hard, I stood up and, enduring the violent pain, I walked to the door and held onto its frame with both hands. Ah, the stairs had disappeared! The twenty-fourth floor was suspended in midair with nothing below! The elevator cage was still across from us, but could an elevator still be in it? The wind carried the sound of Uncle Lou talking.

"Don't look everywhere indiscriminately. It will blur your vision. There are too many things in this building. You should sit down in the room and listen more."

Limping, I returned to the room and sat down. A sentimental feeling gushed from my heart. I don't remember how many years I had wanted to leave home and go to the temple at West Mountain to study martial arts and live an impoverished, meaningful life. Year after year passed, and I could never fulfill my long-cherished wish (because the mountain was far away, because I had no self-control, and because of feelings for my family). From the time I was a child, I had admired the knights errant who could leap onto rooftops and vault over walls and had looked forward to the day when I could also be as skilled. Later on, I learned that this skill was called "martial arts," and thus I lived for the day when someone would teach me martial arts. But to study martial arts, one had to go to West Mountain—as far away as the ends of the earth. The train ride took four days and four nights. It was also a rocky mountain with no vegetation. Only by taking a concealed path could one reach the temple on the mountaintop. One of my cousins wanted to study the martial arts, too: he went to West Mountain and then returned, saying he had strolled around for a week in the foothills without ever locating the path up the mountain. He saw someone appear in the middle of the mountain and also saw someone emerge from the mountain, but he was unable to find the path. Later, he abandoned the idea of studying martial arts. I also abandoned the idea several years ago because my legs began aching for no reason; it wasn't arthritis, nor was it rheumatism. My legs just started hurting, and as time went on, the pain grew worse and worse.

Sitting and sweating in this sauna-like room, I closed my eyes and thought back to some long-ago events. Whenever I recalled something, my legs felt a little more comfortable. Of course, I was listening at the same time. That person's footsteps were distinct and steady: Could he be a Shaolin martial arts disciple from West Mountain? In my excitement, I opened my eyes. I wanted to ask Uncle Lou. Ah, Uncle Lou was no longer on the windowsill, nor was he in the room. Had he gone downstairs? I hadn't heard him go down. Had he floated out from the window? I went to the door again and peeped out. What I saw was still the view of the room in suspension. I took several cautious steps forward, and at once I was frightened into crawling down. I didn't have the courage to stride out toward midair; even if I had studied Shaolin kung fu, I probably wouldn't have dared. It was too dangerous; I had to rush back inside. I climbed back to the room, stood up, and brushed the dust from my clothes. Just think: this building was twenty-four stories high! I was listening to that person's footsteps. And I wanted more and more to meet him. He couldn't be around other people just because he was ugly? This made no sense. How could Uncle Lou have said this?

"Uncle Lou! Uncle Lou!" I shouted.

After a while, a feeble voice answered me. It was as if the voice were coming from a tunnel to the door. "Don't shout . . . Don't . . ."

It certainly wasn't Uncle Lou's voice. Perhaps it was his nephew from the countryside answering me?

"Uncle Lou!" I shouted again.

"Don't shout . . . Watch out—it's dangerous . . ."

The person was on the stairs, which is to say he was in midair. Judging by his voice, he must be hanging in midair. I couldn't bear to shout again, because I was afraid he would fall. Maybe the one facing danger wasn't he, but I. Was he saying that I was in danger? I didn't dare shout again. This was Uncle Lou's home. Eventually, he would have to return. Perhaps he had simply gone downstairs to buy groceries. It was a nice day. The sun was out, so it was a little hot in the room. So what? I shouldn't start making a fuss because of this. When I recalled that someone outside was hanging in midair, I started sweating even more profusely. My clothes stuck to my body; this was hard to endure. Since there was nothing to see outside, to while away the time I looked closely at the furnishings in the room. I started with Uncle Lou's wooden bed.

Next to Uncle Lou's pillow, besides a flashlight, there was a deck of cards! It looked familiar: it was just like the deck of cards I had lost long ago. I rubbed my sweaty hands on my clothes and went over and picked up the cards. My hands were shaking a lot, and my memory returned to that long-ago afternoon. Ah, it occurred to me that it was Uncle Lou who had stolen them! That old man wearing sneakers and standing in the shadows behind the mosquito net: Who else could it have been? He had taken my treasured deck of cards! So many years had passed, and I had never suspected him, because I thought he was too serious a person to be interested in a plaything like this. These cards had yellowed a little and smelled of the past. Now it was hard to find these old-style cards, which were so simple and enchanting. Look at this black joker: the small mark I'd made on top of it with a ballpoint pen, in case someone stole it, was still visible! Wow, my dear Uncle Lou, I don't know what to say about you!

I put the cards next to the pillow again. I wasn't feeling as agitated anymore, and I was no longer sweating. I steeled myself to look out the window again. Although the sky was still a vast expanse of whiteness, the sun now looked the way it usually did. I don't know why, but I felt that a certain something had already occurred, and so for some reason, I was no longer so worried. Since that kind of thing had happened more than ten years ago, there must also be a reason for what was happening now. I should just wait; I shouldn't worry for no reason. Listen, the footsteps were still there. The nephew who had come from the countryside and couldn't see me was so composed. Now he had actually come upstairs. Truly, he was standing at the door and stamping his feet to knock the mud from his shoes. He was going to come in right away. I went over and opened the door.

It was Uncle Lou. Uncle Lou had come back from grocery shopping. He put down the groceries and suddenly stared at the deck of cards on the bed. With an understanding smile, he said: "You noticed. That's an antique that I packed away long ago! My nephew has left."

Uncle Lou had changed again to the Uncle Lou he used to be. He was merrily cooking on the gas stove as he related some neighborhood gossip. I walked over and helped him wash the vegetables. When I turned on the faucet, some slippery little creatures streamed into the sink. Before I had time to get a good look at them, they had gone down the drain. Filled with irritation,

I was staring at the few stalks of celery. Behind me, Uncle Lou started laughing.

"This neighborhood is 'a Village in the Big City.' There are little fish and tadpoles everywhere, as well as leeches and schisto-somes. We grew accustomed to them long ago."

The water was muddy, and it also smelled like mud. Could it be that this water didn't come from a water tank but from a ditch in the countryside? This was really a weird residential block. I recalled that when I had arrived this morning, I hadn't seen a single person around. It seemed the people all stayed in their own homes. It was more than ten years ago that Uncle Lou had first wanted to close himself off from others. He had wanted to move here to isolate himself from all of us. I realized, however, that in these years he was still closely connected with us. I couldn't offer any proof of this, but the atmosphere in this room—the various odd phenomena—hinted at the attention Uncle Lou gave us. This kind of attention might not please people—sometimes it even felt eerie—but I couldn't deny its presence. While I was watching him cook, a scene from years ago appeared in my mind—the pair of "Liberation" sneakers on the ground. I came to a shocking con-clusion: Uncle Lou was everywhere!

After I washed the vegetables, Uncle Lou told me to sit down and rest. I had no sooner taken a seat than I heard footsteps on the stairs. The nephew hadn't left, after all.

"Who's coming up the stairs?" I asked.

"Who else could it be? He's no stranger to you. If you don't believe me, take a look. It's always like this. They all want to come to my place, but they aren't brave enough. You are. Hedgehog, go to the door and take a look."

Once again, I went over to the stairs. This time, the elevator on the right side was just going down. Maybe the person had taken the elevator. No, someone was still on the stairs. He was my former classmate, the one who had frequently come over to play cards. We hadn't seen each other for a long time. He was a little flustered and fled downstairs. I understood a little—probably people were always going up and down the stairs; maybe they couldn't make up their minds or maybe they liked this sort of activity. The one I'd heard before certainly wasn't indecisive, because his footsteps sounded composed. Were they also fearful of being suspended?

When we sat down to eat, a face appeared at the door. It looked like a farmer, a rough guy who was about thirty or forty years old. Uncle Lou said this was his nephew. Curious, I wanted to get a good look at him. But he turned around and went down the stairs. I thought to myself, this person isn't actually ugly; his features are very ordinary. You could see farmers like this anywhere. But Uncle Lou said that his nephew didn't come in because he was "terribly ashamed of his appearance." I said I didn't think he was at all ugly. Uncle Lou said it was useless for other people to say whether he was ugly or not, for his relative knew himself. Uncle Lou said he had known his nephew since he was little: How could he be mistaken?

I had a brainstorm and steeled myself to ask:

"Then, Uncle Lou, was it for the same reason that you distanced yourself from everyone back then?"

Uncle Lou snorted a noncommittal "Huh." Just then, his nephew reappeared at the door; still smiling, he revealed a mouthful of white teeth. I wanted to go over and greet him, but he ran off again. I told Uncle Lou about being unable to touch my face when I got up in the morning. Listening gravely, Uncle Lou kept nodding his head. I don't know why, but—all of a sudden—in this midair where I couldn't see the surrounding scenery, I couldn't get a grip on my narration. Was I telling him about a real incident or was I making up a story? But it couldn't be just an illusion that this morning, dragging my lame legs, I had climbed up to the home of this Uncle Lou whom I hadn't seen for more than ten years. I had come here specifically to tell him about this: Shouldn't it be absolutely true? Hadn't I transferred buses twice on the way over here? After Uncle Lou heard my story, he shifted his gaze to the air and said blandly:

"You need to exercise."

"How?" I asked nervously.

"Put the mirror under your pillow, and take it out every morning and look in it. You'll grow accustomed to this, and then you'll be all right."

"But I don't want to look in the mirror. You have no idea: it's a terrible feeling."

"Then don't look."

I hadn't expected Uncle Lou to answer me so irresponsibly. In the past, he'd been a considerate old man. Whenever any of us encountered anything frustrating, we all liked to complain about it to Uncle Lou. Not only did he listen attentively, but he also gave us advice.

After we'd finished the meal and the tea, I stood up, intending to take my leave, but Uncle Lou urged me to sit down and said:

"It's going to rain hard. If you leave now, you'll get thoroughly drenched."

Pointing out the window, I said, "It's a nice day." But Uncle Lou still shook his head and said that if I left now, the next morning I'd be even unhappier, because I still hadn't straightened out my thinking. That was true. I had failed to gain strength from Uncle Lou to relieve my inner crisis. What should I do?

Just then, Uncle Lou asked me if I'd like to sit on the windowsill and look at the scenery with him. He added that he enjoyed this more than anything else in life. With that, he sat on the windowsill. He exerted himself to maneuver one side of his body so it was hanging in midair, and he made swimming motions. Seeing this was terrifying, and I didn't dare go up to the windowsill: it was too dangerous. This was also the first time in my life that I had come to such a high place, and the glare from the rays outside the window was intense. As I stood there hesitating, the nephew came in quietly and whispered to me, "I'd really like to push my uncle down. But I'm not strong enough. I . . . I'm a good-for-nothing!" He sat on the floor, and held his head in his hands in agony. This nephew was probably about my age, but his hair had turned gray. He smelled of standing grain, giving me a favorable impression of him. But I couldn't get any handle on this screwball's mood. He actually wanted to push his uncle down from the twenty-fourth floor! Perhaps this idea had been gnawing at him all along. The nephew gave a loud sigh. His uncle made a *hey, hey* sound, as if he would fly out from the window. Uncle Lou seemed overjoyed!

After a while, I heard the gentle sound of rain in the air and smelled its scent, but I couldn't see any rain. I reached my hand out the window, but no rain fell on my hand. The nephew was also taking in the scent of rain, and he was now in a better mood. He stood up and brushed the dust off his clothes. As he walked to the door, he said:

"I've been really happy today!"

After he left, Uncle Lou came down from the windowsill. The old man appeared energetic and invigorated. The sound of rain still came from outside, not the sound of rain falling on the rooftop but the sound of rain in the air: you had to listen quietly in order to hear it. It was like the sound of moths' wings flapping. I saw that half of Uncle Lou's body was drenched. He was changing out of his wet clothing and rubbing his hair with a towel. Because I didn't believe this, I stretched my hand out the window again, but I still felt no rain.

"If you go downstairs now, you'll get soaked through!" Uncle Lou said.

"What about your nephew? Isn't he afraid of being caught in the rain?"

"He looks forward to it. He came to the city from the country-side two years ago and lives in a basement room. You also noticed this: he's very happy . . . If he weren't ugly, he'd be running wild."

"But I don't think he's ugly."

"That's because you didn't get a good look at him."

Although I couldn't see the rain, I could feel that the room had cooled off. Uncle Lou asked me to "go for a walk" with him on the stairs. He said that when we were finished walking, the rain would have stopped.

This time, the stairs were steady and solid under my feet. The illusion of hanging in the air had disappeared. But apparently afraid that I would fall, Uncle Lou kept a tight grip on my arm. He said that he frequently slipped on the stairs because this kind of staircase was treacherous. When Uncle Lou walked downstairs, he was in high spirits. He started talking to me about events of more than ten years ago. I was excited, too, and wanted to talk with him about the past. All of a sudden, I realized that I didn't know anything he was talking about. For example, he said there was a zoo outside the entrance to our home, and the panthers had escaped from the zoo and wandered back and forth on the street. He said he had gone fishing one day and had caught a human head: it was a murder case. He said a circus had come to town. The performers were all spies whose mission was to steal the state's top secrets. He said that one day when I went fishing, I'd forgotten to lock the door. As a result, a thief had stolen a priceless treasure—a rock ink-stone that had been passed down from antiquity. As he talked on and on, I had no idea how long we walked. The stairs descended endlessly. Where were we going? Had we already walked out of the "Village in the Big City" and reached the underground? I didn't ask Uncle Lou, for I was afraid of interrupting his stories. These were the stories I liked best. When Uncle Lou and I walked down another floor, I noticed an open door. I saw the family members celebrating some kind of ritual around a circular table. I didn't have time to get a good look before leaving. Later, I saw the same thing in another home, and then in a third home, and a fourth. Uncle Lou said the people in this building were all noble-minded people. If I came here often, I would realize this.

"Hedgehog, as soon as you arrived, I started feeling remorseful. During these years I think I let you drift around by yourself. You must have been so lonely. Hedgehog, you won't blame me, will you? I did this for your own good."

I told Uncle Lou that I didn't blame him at all. Even though we hadn't seen each other for so long, I had always considered him someone I could rely on. That I had now sought him out proved this. Except for Uncle Lou, I had no other true family in this world. As he listened, Uncle Lou alternately nodded and shook his head. I didn't know if he agreed with me or not. Suddenly, he shoved me aside with one hand and said:

"You wretch: you still haven't altered your basic parasitic nature! Do you want to depend on me forever? Listen, the rain has stopped. You should go home. As for me, I'm going to stop here and visit for a while."

With that, he left me and went to the home on the right. I heard him bolt the door from within.

I'd been left on the stairs by myself. I must have gone down seventy or eighty flights of stairs. Why was it that I still couldn't see the bottom? Scared, I turned around and climbed up. My legs were really supporting me. Nothing was wrong with them. I had never been as strong as now! In the stillness, I climbed and climbed. The afternoon scene from the past kept flashing through my mind. It was always that obscure wing room, and always with the four childhood friends. We were crowded around the small stool where the deck of cards lay. The deck of cards lay on a square stool, and the four of us were crowded around the square stool. Outside, it was raining. Uncle Lou's silhouette flashed out from behind the mosquito net and disappeared out the door . . .

Ultimately, I never found the exit and I returned to Uncle Lou's home. His nephew greeted me at the door.

"Hedgehog, you're back from your walk. You must feel great."

"No, I'm feeling a little depressed. I want to go back to my own home."

As I said this, I was taken aback: How had I become "Hedgehog"? He was my twin brother. In the past, when we lived in the old house, we had been inseparable. It was my brother who had scraped together enough from our pocket money to buy the deck of cards: he was a boy with ideas. Over the years, I had gradually rid myself of the shadow of his death. I had never expected that both Uncle Lou and his nephew would think I was Hedgehog.

"You've already been gone fourteen years. What difference does it make if you go back a little later?"

Ah, he still thought I was Hedgehog!

"I'm Puppy."

"We know you're Puppy."

When he said this, I suddenly noticed that his face had become scary, just like a leper's. He looked as if he would throw himself at me, so I turned around right away and ran off. I ran to the elevator; its door opened automatically. It was empty. I closed the door and quickly pushed the button for the first floor. The elevator was slow, and, staggering, it finally stopped. As soon as the door opened, I streaked outside. The sun was bright, so dazzling that I couldn't open my eyes. When I passed the gate guard, I heard the middle-aged man say loudly:

"Isn't this Hedgehog from Old Qin's family? How did he happen to come to our 'Village in the Big City'?"

The others burst into loud laughter. I flushed, but I didn't know why they were laughing.

I walked to the main street, and turned around to look at the

"Village in the Big City." Uncle Lou and his nephew were standing at the entrance waving to me. They looked reluctant to see me go, but as soon as I recalled the nephew's hidden ugly face, I began trembling. The cars going back and forth blocked their images, and I continued walking ahead. I walked for a long time. The three twenty-four-story residential buildings were still behind me. If I turned around, I would see the compound. It was so close that I could even see Uncle Lou's small room. I picked up my pace, but after a while I couldn't help looking back again. Ah, a bamboo pole was sticking out from Uncle Lou's window. What game was he playing? Was he greeting me? I waved and hurried on.

Sitting in the bus, I heard the following conversation:

"This rain was really heavy; it's never rained so hard before. The tadpoles in your pond all swam over to my side . . ."

"Yes, it rained really hard, welcoming us home."

"When you left, did you put the playing cards away?"

"Someone did it for me. They're safe."

I opened my eyes and saw two men who looked like farmers in front of me, but they certainly didn't seem to be the ones who had just been talking. My staring made them unhappy, and I hurriedly shifted my gaze.

I transferred to another bus and went home. The first thing I did when I went inside was to see if the small mirror was still under the pillow. It was. I looked in the mirror several times. Nothing was wrong.

I sat at the table and recalled today's adventure. I felt that my innermost being had been substantially enriched. Perhaps I should start calling on Uncle Lou frequently. It was about time. "Village in the Big City": what a marvelous name!

When she arrived, it was already three in the morning, a time when the lights were all out in the apartments in this old building. I heard her coming up the stairs, and then she entered my apartment. She must have walked through half the city to get here—I figured she lived in the suburbs. It was a little absurd that someone like me chose to live in the downtown area. Even though the room was so dark, I saw her long hair glistening. Where was the light coming from? As always, she stood in the middle of the room, giving off a slight smell of dried red peppers. When I asked her to let me stroke her hair, she walked over and bent down in front of me. Her hair was like a horse's mane, icy cold and vigorous. I couldn't help burying my face in it.

"Can you see me?" I asked.

"Of course. But I'm not accustomed to using my eyes. Where I live, we have lots of things to play with—as many as the cockroaches you have here, layer after layer of them . . ."

"Are there cockroaches in my room?"

"Yes. They're under the floor struggling to emerge. The city is the cockroaches' kingdom. Where I live it's different; we have different things—like clouds floating in the air, sometimes dense and sometimes sparse. When they are extruded too densely, they usually discharge sparks that make *pih-pah pih-pah* sputtering sounds. When I'm there for a long time, I get scared, so I've come to you. Give me your hand, okay?"

Her mouth was ice-cold, gripping my palm like an acetabulum. My hand tingled. She asked me what it felt like, and I said I was a little afraid but it didn't matter. It was always better not to be alone. I also asked her what she'd seen on her way here. She said it seemed there'd been some white mice, but she hadn't seen them. She'd figured this out from the shape, because one had jumped onto her breasts.

She suddenly leapt from the bedside and then squatted. I heard sharp teeth biting sand. The light on her black hair flickered.

"Elena (this was the foreign name I had given her), may I go to your home?"

"No. The air there is too thin. Your lungs couldn't take it."

"Aren't you afraid of cockroaches?"

"Yes, I am. But you're here. You're a man, and I love you."

She curled up into a ball under the table. She looked like a little bear, a little bear nibbling on quartz. She looked sweet.

A lot of noise started coming from the streets, as if a powerful army were hurrying past. This sort of thing didn't occur very often—probably only once or twice a year. She just sat there, aloof and indifferent. The *chachacha* . . . *chachacha* was rhythmic. I asked when she had started loving me, and she said a long time ago.

"At that time, there was nothing frightening where we lived. My parents and my five brothers swam around all day long. As for me, I stood at the window and yearned for you."

"Back then, I probably wasn't in the picture, was I?"

"Possibly. Then you appeared later. I remember that I first saw you at the small coal pit. I often went there and listened closely to how those people emerged from the ground. You were the last one to come out. I heard your whole body make a tiny sound; perhaps it was discharging electricity. This was eight years ago. My parents also knew about you and me. They said this was a good thing. My parents and my brothers often bring this up to make fun of me."

It grew quiet outside. Hand in hand, Elena and I went downstairs. The street lights were on, and we kissed under the moonlight. It rained yesterday, so the streets were clean, and they didn't look at all as if an army had just passed by. Skipping and leaping, she started running off. Her long hair was like a torch. I wanted to chase her, but I couldn't catch up. Turning the corner, she disappeared without a trace. Ah, I heard a lot of people opening their windows to look at me.

When I went upstairs, I saw some cockroaches in the corridor. Some were even flying back and forth in the lamplight. In the daytime, we couldn't see them. Our building was well-known in this city for its cleanliness and comfort. No one living in the building had seen Elena here at night. They said I walked in my sleep; maybe this was the building's fault. Once in the daytime, when I had introduced Elena to a few of the other residents, they all said she was a cashier in a nearby supermarket. "She's really a vivacious girl."

———

Because I persisted, Elena had to agree to take me to her home. Sure enough, she lived in the suburbs. Although it was a fine day, she told me to wear a raincoat and boots. I countered, asking her why she wasn't wearing them. She said she didn't get sick easily, for she was accustomed to the wind and rain. She also said that even though I had worked in the small coal pit, I was very frail. Because I couldn't foresee what I might run into, I deferred to her.

That place wasn't the one I used to be familiar with. I recall that not long after we set out, we crossed an overpass. From there, we made several turns in small alleys. Soon, I no longer recognized anything. It seemed to be a densely settled residential area. The paths between the buildings were crowded with peddlers selling all kinds of things; most of their goods were made of plastic. The peddlers were hawking their wares, and it was so crowded that one couldn't walk through. Elena was very agile, wriggling her way like a snake through the goods and the peddlers. Soon, she disappeared. Worried, I shouted hoarsely: "Elena! Elena!" When I bumped into and overturned a booth, the peddlers pushed me to the ground and trampled on me. Everything before me turned black.

Everything around me changed. I didn't know if I was having trouble with my eyes or if the sky had really darkened; everything became indistinct. I smelled a bad odor, like rotting garbage in the kitchen. I struggled to sit up. My hand pushed against the slimy ground. I lifted my hand to my nose; it was smelly and disgusted me so much that I tried hard to stand up. Had they thrown me down next to the cesspit? After examining it carefully for a moment, I decided it wasn't like a cesspit. It must still be the residential district. No lights were on in the houses, and it didn't seem as if anyone was there. Needing a place to wash my hands, I walked into the nearest building. I made a sound that horrified me: "Elena?!" It didn't occur to me that a small, scalding hand would reach out and take my hand. It was she!

"Elena, I have to wash my hands. They're stinky."

"Don't bother."

She dragged me into a room and told me to squat down.

"My brothers are next door. Don't make a sound. I'm afraid they'll laugh at me."

I squatted down and subconsciously touched the floor with my hands. Ah, it, too, was slippery and smelly.

"Did someone spill dung in this room?" I asked.

Elena didn't answer. I sensed that she was trying hard to hold back a snicker. I was annoyed.

From outside the door came the sound of heavy footsteps. After a while, they went past.

"That was my parents. They love me very much. You were hurt;

do you want to lie down? There's no bed here. The damned peddlers have moved them all out. Do you want to lie down on the
floor?"

"No!"

"Ah, you're still not used to our place. Although the vendors
are a little loathsome, their intentions are good. And, after all,
didn't you come here to experience my life? They're helping you."

"This place is really disgusting."

"Shh. Don't talk so loud! That's because you aren't used to it
yet. I'll get something for you to look at it. It will surprise you."

In a corner, she made a *ka, ka, ka* noise, as if she were cutting
sandstone with a knife. Her small form was hopping around like
a tiny squirrel. I thought, such a pretty girl actually lives in this
kind of environment. But she seemed satisfied with it. When she
went to my apartment, her whole body emitted a spicy scent. I
jokingly called her "Aster." What was this all about? Ah, she came
over.

She placed something in my hand. It was like a cobblestone—icy,
round, and smooth, but something inside it was shaking slightly.
I nervously pinched it and waited for something else to happen.

Someone in the hallway called her, pronouncing her name very
strangely. I couldn't understand. Jumping up, she left at once. I
guessed that it was her brothers who had called her. She had told
me that she and her brothers had cut a hole in the craggy cliff. I
got the impression that these brothers were very fierce.

The round stone I was holding shook more and more violently.
I couldn't hold onto it, and it fell onto the muddy floor, where
it wailed in pain like a baby. I picked it up at once. It became
immobile; it had probably died. I had actually caused it to die.
What would Elena think of me? I was really a good-for-nothing! I
put the stone in my pocket and groped my way to the door.

They were arguing outside. Those men wanted to drive me
away, but Elena disagreed. Raising something like a whip, they

thrashed her. As she was being lashed with the whip, she jumped around and screamed, the sound as tragic as the sound the stone had just made. In my anxiety, I threw the stone at them. The three of them were nonplussed, and an even stronger smell arose.

"Him??" one of the men said.

I didn't have time to say a word before they all ran off. I heard Elena laughing.

"Are they your brothers?"

"Yes. You're really brave!"

Bending down, she picked up the stone and returned it to me. Alive again, the stone was shaking. We walked toward the room.

"What is this?"

"It's something my brothers and I found in the lower grotto. There are many of them. We cut it with a machine and burnished it into several round stones."

"Since you gave it to me, does that mean I'm now one of you?"

"You're really smart."

"I'd like to see that grotto."

"No one knows where it is. We fell into it from a high place. No one wants to fall a second time. Hurry up and put this on!" She handed me a large bamboo hat.

I had no sooner put the hat on than those damp things started falling from above. They became denser and denser, just like a downpour. I thought, this must be night-soil.

"Above us is a place for raising ducks. All the ducks are raised hanging in the air. It's time for them to defecate now."

"This layout of this building is really bizarre."

As I was dragging her along to hide in the hallway, I noticed that her clothes were dry. Although I was surrounded by a stinky smell, I smelled a faint scent of cinnamon coming from her.

"You said earlier that it was clean here. You said it was like clouds floating in the sky. Why did you make this comparison? It's nothing like that."

"Everything I said is true."

"If I come back, I won't be able to find you. I don't remember anything about how to get here," I grumbled. "And I'm covered with shit. It's so stinky; don't you think I'm disgusting?"

She snickered again. I heard her. She said she would take me to "the place where she hides."

"The place where she hides" wasn't in her home, but in a large chicken coop outside the house. It had no door: she and I could both enter it by bending over. Probably several dozen mother hens were in there; illuminated by faint moonlight, the hens all looked seriously ill. Not at all surprised by our arrival, they quickly made room for us. Elena and I squatted on top of chicken shit; if it had been daytime, we would have looked very silly. In her fleece coat, she looked much like a little lamb. She told me, "They've arrived." I asked her who; she said it was the clouds. I couldn't get a good look at her, but I knew her eyes were closed. With her face upturned, she looked intoxicated with happiness. I tried to do exactly what she was doing, but to no avail. Just then, something happened: the stone in my pocket made a big commotion. When I took it out, it quivered violently.

"You need to pinch it tightly," Elena said gently.

But after a while, it slipped out of my hand again. No sooner had it fallen down than the mother hens all went crazy and flew around in confusion. They even fiercely pecked my face a few times. My face was bleeding. If I hadn't covered my eyes with my hands, they would have even pecked out my eyeballs. Annoyed, Elena dragged me out of the chicken coop, but she didn't forget to pick up the stone. I heard her say: "You're really mischievous. Stop for a moment, okay?" She put the stone—now calm again—back into my hand.

"Once a stone is picked up by someone in that kind of place, the stone is doomed to have no peace."

She said that now there was no place we could stay. We could only take the desperate step of going to a place called "Stockaded Mountain Village." We certainly couldn't stay here: I heard her brothers in the dark room shouting her name with that strange pronunciation. They sounded like devils. She was holding my arm tightly, more or less dragging me between houses. The path was full of discarded wood and garbage cans. All of a sudden, she stopped in the middle of the road and said we had reached the stockaded mountain village. Next to us was a large heap of dark things: Elena said it was a bear. But that thing didn't look at all like a bear: it was roughly as large as half a cabin.

"I love to lean against it and think of that matter. When I lean against it, this place becomes so open. There are only some clouds. From a distance, my parents and brothers call to me and I call to them. You may shake hands with it."

Reluctantly, I extended my hand to the dark thing. Although I didn't touch anything, when I pulled my hand back, I heard a light popping sound, as if there were suction there.

"You touched it, didn't you? What do you think of it? This is our stockaded mountain village—its and mine. My family members can't find this place. If they hadn't driven me out, I wouldn't have brought you here, either." Her voice was filled with furtive joy.

Inspired by her words, I extended my hand to it time and again and listened repeatedly to the popping sound. I even walked into it, but there was nothing inside. Of course, there were some things, because I felt the buoyancy of the air, and indeed, my feet kept leaving the ground and falling to the ground again. Elena's voice was now far away.

"Two flowers, three flowers. Ha. I see too many . . ."

I wasn't very accustomed to the buoyancy of the air. I kept wanting to grab something to steady myself. There was a lamp post. I would hang onto it. My movement caused me to fall head over heels, and it was hard to turn around. When I looked again,

I couldn't see any street light; there was just a faint streak of light, that's all. Elena's voice still reached me now and then.

"It's high . . . Drop down . . . Go home!"

Was she telling me to go home? But I didn't want to go back. The air all around had become so clear and fresh and cool, and it was emitting the fragrance of narcissi. If I were just a little patient and didn't get flustered, I wouldn't fall. And even if I fell, I wouldn't die from it. I still wanted to stay a while longer and see if anything had changed here. I began making slow breast strokes, but they weren't nearly as smooth as in the water. Any slight over-exertion would send me tumbling over and over again. It would be much better if it were too dark to see anything: that way, I could follow my own inclinations. This half-light, half-dark atmosphere meant that I needed to be particularly cautious, because obstacles lay everywhere. It was impossible to decide whether you had to deal with them seriously. Most of the obstacles were illusory, like that lamp post.

After I entered Elena's stockaded village, the stone in my pocket calmed down. When I brought it to my ear, I could still hear the buzzing sound; it was steady and joyful. For the moment, it seemed I had no way to leave her stockaded village. I tried to, but I just couldn't. Anyhow, now I didn't want to go, for this place was refreshing. Ah, if Elena were here, it would be wonderful! We could perform a moon-walking dance together, or we could embrace and kiss one another in the sweet-scented air current. I saw huge shadows edging toward me—three of them altogether. Maybe they were the cloud-like things she had talked of. They finally came over and wrapped me up in them. Actually it wasn't frightening; it was just a little darker. This is what I thought at first. Later, when it grew darker and darker, and I heard the sound of grinding and sparks bursting forth all around me, I grew nervous.

"Elena! Elena!" I shouted.

"Go home . . . go home . . ."

Her voice was splintered by the wind—a little here, a little there. I couldn't distinguish what direction it was coming from. These three things were probably all grinding against each other, and I might become a sacrificial lamb. She told me to go home, but how could I break out of here? I closed my eyes and collected my thoughts and continued to swim in one direction. I warned myself to take it easy and not to be worried or rash. I remembered that in the beginning Elena hadn't wanted me to intrude on her world: perhaps I was as curious about her as she was about me. Now I heard the sound of something detonating next to me: I was both excited and frightened. How long had I been swimming? Why hadn't I already made my way out of the stockaded village? I'd better open my eyes.

The mountain really did appear before me. The mountain was filled with the wandering beams of torches. I thought I would swim over to that side. I tried hard, and then harder, but it was useless: I was still in the same place. The wind made my raincoat puff up and my feet left the ground. Someone next to me was talking, his voice growing louder and louder.

"We more or less understand the circumstances over there. You've seen it, too. This kind of mountain always collects energy . . . What does it rely upon? It's nothing but mutual extrusion . . ."

Ah, it was Lai. I had already walked to the end of the alley, and the rain was coming down hard. Lai winked at me and said: "You dunce—wandering around at night in this kind of weather!"

I knew he was suggesting that I was sleepwalking. I wasn't angry with him. I didn't mind. I felt my pocket: the stone was still there. I stumbled a little, but I still took it out. The rain moistened it.

"Put it away. I have one of these stones, too!"

He began to run and reached our building before I did. He entered.

When I went upstairs, it was suddenly light. The corridor was clean. Looking at myself again, I saw that I was clean, too. When I went into my room, I took off my raincoat and placed the stone on the table. Then, looking in the mirror, I combed my messy hair. While I was doing all these things, I kept one eye on the stone. It became an ordinary stone. I brought the stone to my ear. There was no sound at all. All of its life force had slipped away.

Without knocking, Lai came in furtively.

"Do you really have a stone like this?" I asked, a little disappointed.

"Hunh. Whoever wants one can pick one up."

"Where?"

"I'm not too sure, but anyhow, inside a grotto. Many people have fallen into it. In rainy weather like this, who wouldn't want to get out? I understand you. I've come to talk with you about the mountain."

Lai was an idler in this old building. I had rarely heard him talk so earnestly. What he was saying startled me. He sat down comfortably on the recliner, but he didn't talk with me about the mountain. Because he was in charge of collecting the water fees for this building, I went to get the money for him. I had taken only a few steps before I stopped in amazement: the grinding, as well as a slight sputtering, began to sound in the room. Both sounds were coming from Lai's mouth. I recalled what Elena had said: "Like clouds floating in the air. Sometimes dense and sometimes sparse. They make *pih-pah pih-pah* sputtering sounds." I raised my voice: "Where is the mountain? Is it raining on the mountain, too?"

Lai jumped up, saying, "You fool, you fool," and hurriedly left.

It was broad daylight. I had nothing to do. I felt time hanging heavy on my hands. I wanted to revivify myself. I took a cold shower and did thirty push-ups. Then I rushed outside with my umbrella. I ran straight to the end of the street, turned onto another street, ran to the end of it, and then ran home. While I was running, heavy rain fell onto my umbrella like a chorus: "Elena! Elena!"

I belong to the moonlight; the lion belongs to the darkness. The strange thing is that the lion is always walking back and forth, bathing in the moonlight in the wasteland, and I am generally tilling the humus soil with the earthworms. I only till, never harvest. Sometimes, I work my way out of the ground to stand beside the shrubs and wait. When a bat stops to rest, I jump onto her back. Then, carrying me, she flies to the ancient cave. I don't want to describe my experience in the dark cave: it's a place eerier than hell. Even in the daylight, every now and then the tragic cry of slaughter comes from the cave. I wait in the cave until nightfall, when my friend carries me on her back and flies toward the forest. When she stops on a pine tree, I leap to its highest branch. From there, I look out: the wasteland undulates in my field of vision, and the lion is anxiously looking for food. His objective is the zebra on the opposite shore of the stream; my objective is the lion. But why does he never attack? Does he like the high he gets from being dominant?

It's dark, and my friend has flown off. The branch is swaying in the wind, and I am holding on to the branch, clinging to it with my belly. I imagine myself canoeing in the ocean. The moon has risen, and I see the lion at rest. The zebra is resting, too. Only a shallow stream separates them. How does the lion dispel his hunger pangs? This is his secret, and it is also my secret question. The moonlight dyes his long mane silver. His face is as ancient as the rock beside him. I'm enthralled by his face, but his face also troubles me day and night, because I can't find the solution.

The forest becomes noisy, as usual: in the moonlight, these fellows won't be quiet. There are all kinds of sounds everywhere. Branches crack with a sound so vigorous that it's as if they want to turn the entire forest into ruins. Luckily, there are fireflies here—so many that they stream like waves of stars before my eyes. Some—the wingless ones—pause on the withered leaves on the ground and shine silently. Their light can reflect only a little spot under their feet. These are blind insects. I once tried to lure these wingless fireflies to go with me into the earth. They ignored me; they're too proud. It can also be said that they are complacent and self-sufficient. Their idea is that they till their own bodies. The lion has turned around; his back is to me now: what a sorrowful view it is. Now, even the zebras are in a stupor; trusting to luck, they've entered dreamland.

On vast Mother Earth, silhouettes of some other lions have emerged. They aren't real lions, but a trick of the moonlight. These illusions form a single line, extending to the horizon. Have you heard the lion weep? No, the lion's weeping is inaudible. My vision is blurred, and I'm weary from standing on a high place. I have to go down. Once I'm mixed in with those noisy fellows in the night, I relax, body and soul.

I know that my friend is working right now, so I'd better walk back. I walk a very long time before reaching the land I was tilling. In the moonlight, the large expanse of dark earth looks a little like a gloomy graveyard. A heap of wingless fireflies is assembled below the bosk. What is this all about? Is it some kind of ceremony? The heap of tiny fires was gleaming, and gradually grew dark! They burned up their inner fire beside the land I was tilling. These tiny insects had limited choices. I smelled the charred flesh: the odor left me in a bad mood. From the cave, I burrowed underground. I slept as I tilled. Sometime in the middle of the night, I encountered the earthworms. There were two of them—one above me and one below me, and they kept advancing along with me. It was always like this. I couldn't see the earthworms, and yet they were always with me. As soon as they came toward me, I sensed them at once, for in the depth of the soil, the sensors were subtle. I could even sense their mood. The one above me was brimming with enthusiasm; the one below me was a little depressed. They were both time-tested believers. What did they believe in? They believed in everything, just like me. It was a faith born of the source. We were the moonlight school. The dark field was the place where we carried out our faith. I am going to fall into a dream: I knew I would dream of my grandfather. Neither an animal nor a plant, my grandfather was a little like the ocean's coral. But he was born in a place deep in the earth. In his lifetime, he couldn't move. He was always in the same place, thinking, thinking. After he died, it is said that his body fossilized in the place right under where I'm tilling—deep down, very, very deep. There will always be a day . . .

===

I awakened. It was another day. Without emerging from the ground, I felt the heat from the sun's rays. I was anxious to know how the lion was doing. When I left him the day before, he was weeping. As soon as he wept, my brain went blank. He was so gloomy inside. Why did I care so much about him? Because he was king of the earth? Or was there another reason? Anyhow, my caring for him was connected with my faith: I hadn't chosen this; rather, I had been born with it. I couldn't go out yet, for my skin couldn't stand the sunlight. I had to get a lotus leaf from the pond beside the field and cover my head with it.

As I was swimming in the pond, I saw the corpses of many winged fireflies floating on the surface. Alas, those corpses of the moonlight nearly brought me to tears! I selected a lotus leaf, placed it on my head, and swam to shore. Something in the water pulled at my foot: it was an old fish who lived at the bottom of the pond. I was too weary to go to his home. The old fish was the most boring fellow in the world, and his home wasn't like a home, either: it was no more than a clump of water-weeds in the silt. Most of the day, he was in a daze as he squatted in the clump of water-weeds. He didn't think about anything; he was a fish devoid of any thought. He called me "the tiller"; I knew that was a slight. He also called my work "repairing the globe." "The world can't become square just because you're repairing it," he said. Of course, the old fish was experienced and astute, but his experience and astuteness certainly didn't come from his thought; it came from—how to say it? A certain instinct. He was one step ahead of anything that happened in this pond. For example, when I was still in the field and he knew that I was about to arrive, he overcame his inertia and swam up, squatted in a cave beside the pond, and waited for me to pass by. I wouldn't go to his home; he knew this, but he was still unwilling to give up. Since quarreling with him the year of the hailstorm, I had vowed I would never step foot inside his house. That hailstorm was different from ordinary hailstorms: thickly dotted, egg-sized hail fell for a day and a night, and a thick layer of it piled up in the pond. The old fish hid in an earthen cave next to the pond; the earth caved in and sealed the cave's entrance. He slowly bored his way out; he struggled for two days before escaping. It was only because I felt uneasy that I went into the pond. That day, he and I resorted to staying in the stone cave. I was trembling from the cold; I was almost frozen stiff. In the beginning, we talked about this hailstorm, and then we began arguing, because I was well-intentioned and advised him to move into the stone cave, but he not only wasn't grateful but cursed me for being a "coward." He said he couldn't imagine bamboozling himself. "Where is your home? Isn't it under the pile

of hail? Why don't you go home? Why do you have to hide here?"
I countered. At the time, he kept opening and closing his big
mouth. He must have wanted to refute me, but since he couldn't
think, he didn't know how to do that. The old fish didn't say
anything, but the expression in his eyes terrified me to the core.
It was a steely, bewitching expression. I felt completely defeated
by him. I can't say for sure how he had defeated me, but anyhow,
I had suffered a deadly attack. I was in low spirits for several days.
Luckily, I had my work: tilling was an omnipotent magic device.
It could cure any injuries to the soul.

With the lotus leaf on my head, I streaked ahead. As I ran,
I whooped impudently. If I didn't shout, my body would dis-
solve in the sunlight: I was convinced of this. Finally, I reached
the old poplar tree and concealed myself in the dense branches
and leaves. This was much better for my skin. I climbed up to
the highest branch. The zebra had already left. I heard that the
zebras were just passing by; they were on their way to Africa.
They belonged to the sun. Was it because of this that the lion was
profoundly awed by their stripes? The lion was blocked by a large
rock; I could see only the profile of his head. What was he thinking about? At night, did he launch an attack against the zebras? I
really wanted to shout at him, but I knew that my voice couldn't
carry that far. And besides, he wouldn't pay any attention to me.
When I thought of the animals that he ate, I felt disgusted with
him. I abhorred killing. I—and the earthworms, too—ate only the
earth, and even that we didn't really eat. We merely let the earth
travel through our bodies, that's all. We were benign animals.
Underground, we dreamed of the moonlight and dreamed of our
ancestors. Although he was disgusting, our esteem for the lion
took the upper hand: after all, he was the king who dared to sub-
due Mother Earth. For example, right now: I was watching him
with tears in my eyes. Did I fall in love with him? Nonsense—who
could love a lion? He started moving. He was walking toward the

riverside, and his shadow was thick and black in the sunlight, as though another lion, a black one, were walking behind him. He was drinking water; he drank for a long time. How could he drink for so long? Was he extinguishing an inner fire? An oriole dropped to his head. The little fellow began singing at once; it was such a sweet, clear sound—so resounding! Even I could faintly hear it. The lion stopped drinking water; he was listening, too. He didn't move lest he frighten the little bird. I noticed that while the bird was singing, the lion's shadow disappeared. When the bird stopped singing and flew away, the shadow returned. The lion squatted with his back to the sun, and the shadow circled around in front of him. His image gave me an impression of agony. I wanted to go back, for the moisture on my body had all evaporated; this was very rough on me.

With the lotus leaf on my head again, I scampered off with a whoop. I shouted even more hysterically than I had before, because the sunlight was particularly strong and I was afraid it would spell the end of me. I ran and ran and finally got home. I plunged head-first into the dark cave and stuck my wrinkled skin tightly against the cold, wet earth. I nearly fainted. Not far from me, the earthworms were working systematically. These creatures of the moonlight in fact went their whole lives without seeing the moonlight, but they transmitted messages to me, telling me that they profoundly venerated the moonlight. And so, like me, they were looking into their ancestry. The earthworms' skin was even more fragile than mine. If they encountered sunlight, they would melt into water. It's said that this occurred many times in the past. Then, why did they have to hide even from the moonlight? Why? They didn't tell me.

═══

I regained my strength and began plunging down, down, into a deep spot in the ground. I wanted to till vertically. I had tried this earlier, but I had stopped each time I penetrated to the limestone. It wasn't that I didn't want to continue, but that I couldn't stand the smell. The strange thing was that no matter which direction I took in plunging down, in the end I always arrived at the layer of limestone. I couldn't detour around it. Perhaps it was only a thin layer, or perhaps it was a very deep mineral hell. Either was possible. This time, in desperation, I resolved to risk danger and explore one time. I thought, there must be a way to get through this; otherwise, how had Grandfather and the others made their way down? I didn't believe that he had been born underground. I heard a slight noise behind me: it was the earthworm following me. Him? Following me? This was suicidal! Just think about his skin. I was about to reach that place, and I already had a headache. My rigid eyeballs were also on the verge of softening. Following the course I had set, I circled toward the right. Circling for a long time, I put up with the odor. My eyeballs had already turned extremely turbid: I could see almost nothing. What was this? A natural cave! A tunnel stretching down! This was unexpected. Naturally, I stuck my head inside. It happened that this cave could accommodate my body, so I went on for a while and then grew frightened. Was this a journey with no return? However, it was already too late to return. I had walked so far. If I turned around, I didn't know how many days it would take. It was great that the earthworm behind me kept making noise, as if to boost my courage; otherwise, I would have lost my nerve. Although there was also a limestone odor in the tunnel, it was better than outside. Bit by bit, as my vision was restored, I saw some strange decorative designs on the wall of the cave: they were everywhere. After observing enough of them, I concluded that these were similar designs that were constantly changing places. They were dispatched and re-formed again and again, giving the eyes a constant sense of novelty. These simple, primitive designs took the edge off the dread I was feeling. How could there be this kind of tunnel? How had I happened to find it? Could it be that it was Grandfather's masterpiece? The moisture in my body began bubbling up, and I heard that fellow behind me excitedly grow even noisier. He was beating against the wall of the cave. Each time—in fact, he was rubbing the wall with his head—the wall of the cave made a strange sound, as if it were saying, "That's right, that's right . . ." I felt comforted that he was there—my good friend. Otherwise, I probably would have fainted in disbelief. I don't know how long I crept through the tunnel, because underground there was no distinction between day and night. However, I remember that in those moments the distinction between all things vanished. There was neither any sound nor any image: even the earthworm behind me didn't move. No matter how much energy I expended knocking my head against the wall of the cave, I couldn't make any sound nor could I see anything. Was it possible that this was "death"? But this situation didn't last long. When my ears made a rumbling sound, my feeling came back (was it simply a problem with my feeling?). With each passage I crept along, "death" repeated itself. Later on, I grew used to this. Not only was I no longer afraid, but I even looked forward to it a little. In moments like that, my brain was transformed into an endless ocean. The lion's incomparably huge silhouette appeared; he lay on the blue water. A nightingale flew over behind him. This scene appeared time after time, and I had the illusion that this trip wasn't to find Grandfather, but to find the lion. How could one go underground to find the lion? This was a question that would normally be raised, but I had already abandoned normal logic. I recognized that I was looking for the lion, and planned, too, to talk with him after I found him—even if it meant being eaten by him. I wouldn't mind.

How could I drop down? I thought back on this over and over, and I was still at a loss. At the time, it seemed I had come to the end of the tunnel, for I saw a vast expanse of white. I couldn't grasp whether I had emerged from the ground or whether I was still underground. Much less could I figure out where "up" and "down" were ahead of me. By then, even the earthworm had vanished without a trace. Turning back had become even more impossible. I've already said that this tunnel was so narrow that it was really lucky it could accommodate my body, so there was no way I could turn around at the cave entrance. This was really dangerous, almost the same as finding a pretense to "drop down." Of course, after a long trip, I reached my goal. Was this place really my goal? Where was the lion? Now, even the lion didn't appear on the ocean. It had become a dead sea.

Time kept passing, and I was still in the same place. But how could I stay in the same place forever? I couldn't eat the earth here, for it had a very strong limestone odor. I had never fasted for such a long time. Now, utterly weakened, I was about to faint. Maybe it was in that moment that I made up my mind that I was in for a penny, in for a pound, and I might as well drop down. Just as I was falling, the lion appeared. So large, and yet so agile, he filled my entire field of vision. His mane—ah, his mane . . . Whatever happened afterward, I don't remember. I seemed to be in a murky, rocky hole. Something was swaying in the air—sometimes a foot, sometimes a skull. That was my last memory. Maybe I just couldn't bear to look back at what was happening, and so I forgot it. Sometimes I think that maybe what happened was truly death? Could that rocky hole have been Grandfather's tomb? What could be so unbearable to remember?

Anyhow, when I woke up, I was in my own field. There were earthworms above me and earthworms below me, earthworms to my left and earthworms to my right. They weren't tilling the land; they were quietly waiting for me to wake up. When I woke up and let out a sound, they slowly began their activity. I heard their excitement: their supple bodies were knocking the earth, making a *tili, tili, tili* sound, just like the falling rain. In that instant, I was intoxicated with the sound of rain purifying the soul. I really wanted to break through the layer of earth that separated us and embrace these viscous companions. I wouldn't care if their sticky fluid flowed all over my body. But I didn't, because I knew that neither they nor I were accustomed to expressing ourselves this way. We were introverted creatures, used to communicating our enthusiasm in solitude. How softly and comfortably the earth was clinging to my body! I roused myself to till more than ten meters away from here. My companions were following me. It was as if we were swimming freely in the ocean (naturally, I have to admit that I've never been to the ocean)! Ah, let me till deeper; I wanted to double the size of my field! I tilled vertically again, and my companions kept following me. Some also tilled in front of me. Just as we were tilling enthusiastically, we heard the lion's roar. My companions and I all stopped. It seemed that the sound was coming from a grotto. It shook the soil until it wobbled a little. Had the lion gone underground? I recalled all the scenery I had glimpsed in the moment that I fell down from the entrance of the tunnel. Could it be that the lion had been underground then, and that the lion atop the wasteland had been merely a shadow—one of his many shadows? In the midst of the roaring, we were all silent. We wanted to understand what the roar meant. But after roaring several times, he stopped: we hadn't had time to figure it out. We could only try our best to recall it. As we tried, our brains went blank. This kind of reasoning led to no outcome at all. Then, as if we had made an agreement, we began tilling the land together again. We were dead tired from our work. As I tilled the land, I dreamed about the lion in the grotto. Always, it was that incomparably large head, the silvery mane giving off light like the sun—so dazzling that I couldn't open my eyes. Someone whimpered in my ear: "I can't move." Who? Could it be the lion? Why couldn't the lion move? It was only my grandfather who couldn't move! Then was the lion my grandfather? Ah, my thinking was all mixed up. I couldn't go on thinking, but I still had my feelings and I sensed that he was there, underground, holding his breath, about to explode. I dreamed for a really long time. In my dream, I ate a lot of earth. The *tili, tili, tili* sound enveloped me again. They were knocking again, and I was so moved that I thought I would cry.

When I emerged from the ground again, all the fireflies were dead, moonlight was spread across Mother Earth, and there was a strong funereal odor. I climbed to a limb of the old poplar tree and looked over at the plains. The whole area was deserted, except for the shadow of an occasional bird skimming past. Had the realm of lions lost its master? No. He was still present. It looked as if he were fused with the rock: he was absolutely still. His mane no longer shone; his entire body was tarnished. Had he died? The sound of thunder was gradually rolling closer, and the moon was hidden behind dark clouds. The lion's image was a little blurred. Suddenly, he melted into a bolt of lightning and shot out from behind the rock, breaking through the blackened night air. He illuminated heaven and earth, but he lost his own form. This made me doubt whether his body had ever been real. After the explosive thunder ended, there was another bolt of lightning . . . and another! Both shot out from the rock. Now there wasn't even the sound of thunder. These bolts of lightning turned the sky snow-bright; the moon that now and then showed its face had lost its rays of light and was about to turn almost completely dark.

How presumptuous this was. I couldn't bear to go on watching. I went under the ground. The snow-bright lightning jolted the earth. Really. It was willfully tossing the rocks on the earth, as well as the trees and hills, back and forth. I didn't dare look at it, for if I looked again, I would faint. I closed my eyes and felt my way home. Even though I was underground, I still faintly heard the turmoil on the ground.

I was so weary that I quickly fell asleep. In my sleep, I was plowing the familiar rich, black soil. The earthworms rapped politely toward me to transmit a message: Grandfather was alive again. Deep underground, he had regained life and was growing. In my dream, I was feverish all over. I couldn't hear Grandfather growing, but all of the earthworms did. They told me. This was the first time in my life that I felt profoundly that I—and my companions, too—had become one with the grandfather at the earth's core. Was this because of the lion? I tried my best to imagine, but—no matter what—I couldn't call to mind the lion's face.

When I was at home, I always heard people mention "Gaoling." I got the impression that it was a hill, with several long, narrow little streets leading to it. On the hilltop was this city's largest hospital. People said that Gaoling wasn't far from my home. The streets were filled with small houses and dilapidated old two-story wooden buildings. The residents were mainly poor laborers. Those people could barely afford coal for cooking, so when the children had time they headed for the main street with brooms and dustpans. As soon as they saw a little coal fall from a rickshaw, they rushed over and brushed it into a dustpan. In talking of Gaoling, this is the way the adults referred to it. I grew more and more curious: What on earth was Gaoling like?

As it happened, one Sunday I was buying stationery in the vicinity of Gaoling. After doing that, I took a small, narrow alley to Gaoling itself. The sun was strong that day, and people were all taking cover in their houses. I saw no one on the narrow asphalt road. I was perspiring. I walked straight to the end of the road and still didn't see anyone. After I climbed the hill, the road turned and became a downgrade. I hesitated a little and then decided to turn into the area of small, narrow dilapidated houses. It was next to an adobe house that I walked in, and then I immediately saw a filthy public toilet. After passing the toilet, I came to a home where a mourning hall had just been erected. Hanging in the hall were photos of the deceased:

it was a sweet-looking girl wearing a red scarf. She couldn't have been more than fourteen. The coffin hadn't been carried in yet. I was confused: I'd never seen a funeral for a child. I wanted to stand there and watch, but someone drove me off. Someone's heavy palm struck me on the back. Enduring the pain, I ran off, almost crying.

"She died of meningitis," a girl about my age told me.

She looked like an old hand. She had pigtails, and her hands were rough. You could tell by looking at her that she was used to doing housework.

"I don't dare stay at the mourning hall," she added, haughtily curling her lips.

I lacked the courage to accost the girl. The atmosphere all around was too secretive, and I wanted to get away. Between two adobe houses there was a narrow path that could accommodate only one person. As I was about to take the path, the girl pulled me back. She was strong: she pulled at me until I nearly fell down.

"It's a dead end, you fool."

She wanted me to go with her, and so we circled back to the mourning hall and went past it. Some people were already sitting in the hall: they had begun beating the gongs, and a woman was sobbing. I didn't know if it was her mother or a relative. We hurriedly put the hall behind us. I asked the girl where we were going. She answered, "The hospital." I said I wasn't interested in going to the hospital. She insisted, saying, "The hospital is a lot of fun."

We scrambled up the hill and finally went through a cobweb-like and densely settled residential area, and reached a level place made of concrete. On one side of it was a high wall. The girl said the hospital was inside the wall. I thought the entrance to the hospital was nearby, but we walked a long time. We walked past the level concrete area and then once more came to the street.

We were still at the wall, and we hadn't seen even a trace of the entrance.

"Let's rest for a while." With that, the girl sat down on the ground with her back against the wall. Her head drooped.

I saw her massaging the tiny cracks in her palms. As for me, I was hot and thirsty and wanted to go home.

"The hospital is a lot of fun," she said again, as if she'd guessed what I was thinking.

At last, we saw an old woman selling popsicles. I wanted to buy one, but she waved us away and said she had sold them all. Noticing my disappointment, the girl giggled. She told me there was a gap in the wall just ahead and we could get into the hospital that way.

After walking a little farther, we saw the gap in the wall and made our way through it. Ahead of us was an old five-story structure. It was a mess in front of the building. Piles of glass test tubes, syringes, and rubber tubes were everywhere. Mixed in with them were numerous glass jars filled with dubious objects that looked a little like human organs.

"There are little children, some living and some dead. Don't look! Let's run!" the girl shouted.

She and I ran off together. We ran past several black brick buildings. People were looking out from the windows of each building. These were probably hospital wards. Finally, we reached a garden. The girl threw herself down on the lawn and didn't move. And I sat down beside her. A profusion of roses formed the border. I had never seen such beautiful large roses. Their strong fragrance immediately dispelled my fatigue and thirst. It was very quiet in the garden: even the buzzing of bees was audible. I thought, this must be the place that the girl had said was so much fun. And actually it was great here; I didn't want to leave. I shoved the girl. I wanted her to get up and go with me to enjoy the roses, but she didn't move. And so I circled around the large border several times by myself. It was wondrous—and oh, so pleasant—below the blue sky. The more I looked, the more impatient I was to share this with the girl, so I shoved her again. Finally, she sat up, yawning. Like an adult, she said gravely:

"You fool. Under the flowers are little babies, some living and some dead. You mustn't poke at the flowers as you look at them. Last week, a girl in the hospital was frightened here and . . ."

She broke off, keeping me guessing. I shoved her hard and asked, "And what? What happened to her? Hurry up and tell me!!"

"She died." She curled her lips.

"You're talking nonsense! You're the one who told me this place was a lot of fun." All at once, my heart felt empty.

"It *is* a lot of fun. I didn't lie. Come on, let's go look at the flowers together!"

But I didn't want to go with her. I was afraid she would suddenly part the clump of flowers and make me look at that ghostlike thing. I suggested that we admire the flowers from a distance. Staring at me, she nodded in agreement. Ah, the roses! The roses! In the strong floral fragrance and under the gentle blue sky, I felt that I was in a fairyland! The wards next to the slums were so squalid, and yet a wonderland was hidden here. How could anyone imagine this? It was unusual, too, to have the chance to see such a beautiful lawn—so lush, so green, so clean!

I lay on the lawn, pillowing the back of my head with my hands. It was so pleasant to lie down like this. The girl was standing over me. When she bent down to talk with me, her head looked huge—just like a dustpan.

"Hey, you're resting your head on three little babies. Two of them are dead. One is still alive. You've pinned her legs down."

I jumped up with a rush. I wanted with all my heart to dash out of this garden that was possessed by evil spirits. From behind, she held onto me by my clothes and wouldn't let me go. She even tripped me, wanting to make me fall.

"Look at the flowers, look at the flowers! You aren't looking at the flowers."

I felt wronged, and tears welled up in my eyes and spilled out. Through teary eyes, I saw large roses swirling all over the sky, and so I gradually calmed down. I stood there foolishly and gazed at the roses. The girl surreptitiously placed a soft, cold thing in my hand; she wanted me to hang onto it. Flustered, I threw the thing off and swung my arms for all I was worth. I felt something moist on my hand.

"Why are you so jumpy? It's just a twig!" she said.

The wind stopped blowing, and the roses fell slowly to the lawn—one rose here, another there, trembling as if they were alive. I looked closely at my palm and finally saw that it was clean; nothing dirty was there. So I relaxed and took careful steps to avoid trampling the beautiful roses. The girl's voice echoed in my ears—tender, yet stiff; fervent, yet frosty. Such an unearthly voice—

"In the slums of Gaoling, a girl died next to the hospital, and in the hospital there are borders of roses . . . Shhh. Quiet, quiet! We've come out. Look, here's the gap in the wall."

As the girl and I walked on the blazing asphalt road, it was almost twilight. The old woman selling popsicles had gone home.

We parted at the intersection, each of us surprised by the other's presence.

COTTON CANDY

The thing I love watching most is the swirling cotton candy. The contraption for making it is like a flat-bottomed pan. One puts sugar in it, turns the crank, and after a while, a large shimmering ball emerges; it's like cotton—and like silk, too. Indeed, there's nothing lovelier.

The old woman with bulging eyelids who was selling cotton candy was so absorbed in the operation that she never looked up at us. We crowded around the contraption, staring at it with our mouths watering. We secretly hoped that more and more people would show up to buy cotton candy, so that we could watch longer. Still, this didn't mean that we could eat the cotton candy: the old woman had never been that generous. We stood there to feast our eyes. None of the balls of cotton candy was the same; each one had a special beauty of its own. Only our eyes—kids' eyes—could tell them apart. After the cotton candy was shaken out, the old woman spoke in a sharp, crisp voice to the child who had paid for it: "Here you go!" And then our gazes turned toward the thing in the child's hand. We weren't jealous of him. We shared his enjoyment of the delectable food—with our eyes.

Ah, this lovely thing has run through my entire life! That treasure sparkling in the sunlight, that magic-like spinning, brought me so much joy. At the time, I secretly planned to become a cotton candy vendor when I grew up. This old woman's absorption and calmness while she worked were mystifying. Even with my enthusiasm running so high, I was sometimes distracted—for example, when an old crow flew past, or when my parents yelled at us to go home for dinner. But this old woman: after she set up her "black pot" and her customers lined up in front of this contraption, she lowered her eyes and never looked up. I thought that each ball of cotton candy was so marvelous because it was inseparable from her frame of mind. What kind of person was this old woman with hands like bark?

I've eaten cotton candy just twice. It was the most mystifying experience on earth. When I put that soft, transparent, fluttering white thing in my mouth, it vanished like air. It had no taste. I knew I'd seen that cotton candy was made of sugar, so why didn't it taste sweet? I asked Amei and Aming, but they both laughed at me and said I was "miserable." In my anger, I started ranting and raving, and they ran off.

But the cotton candy that those children ate certainly was flavorful. If they were eating only air, they wouldn't make such a scene in front of their parents, demanding a few pennies to enjoy this kind of thing. I understood them. Maybe something was wrong with my taste buds. Later on, I brazenly asked my parents for a few cents, and this time I bought a small pear-shaped one. I tasted it gingerly. I saw this thing melt little by little on my tongue, and still I tasted nothing. It was so unfair: Had the old woman played a trick on me? It didn't seem so. She treated me the same as everyone else. And, after all, she didn't know me: she had never laid eyes on any of us.

My extreme dismay touched off endless daydreams. If I amassed some capital someday and became a vendor, maybe I could shake cotton candy out of the air. I was excited about my brainchild: at midnight, I smiled happily. I would shake out the most beautiful cotton candy, and it wouldn't be white, either. It would be a color I couldn't even imagine. It would be many times more beautiful than the rainbows in the sky or the coral in the sea. And the flavor certainly would not be a sugary taste, but would be a sweetness that had never existed before. It would be better . . . No, I couldn't imagine what it would be better than.

=====

The old woman finally went bankrupt. She had made so much money every day, how could she have gone bankrupt? I didn't get it. She still came to our street to make cotton candy. Children lined up in an orderly fashion. When the first one in line paid his money, she bent her head and started shaking her contraption. She no longer had any white sugar. She was shaking air. Everyone started guffawing. Distracted for a moment, she brought her other hand—the one that was gripping the money—up to her face and stared at it carefully. The child who had given her the money quickly grabbed it from her and took off. She wasn't angry: she just clutched the crank again and shook the air. She didn't even look at us.

Feeling sorry for her, I rushed home and pilfered a small jar of sugar. I shoved my way through the crowd and placed the jar of sugar on the old woman's chopping board. I had barely turned around when I heard a sound: the old woman had swept the jar to the ground. In a frenzy, the children grabbed the sugar that had fallen on the ground. The old woman was still shaking her contraption, her wooden face expressionless. The children whispered that she'd gone "crazy."

As the days passed, fewer and fewer children crowded around. Finally, no one came any longer to watch her crazy activity. I was the only one who was reluctant to leave, and I observed from one side. Sure, I also ran off sometimes, because I had to help out at home and because of other temptations. But for some reason, I kept thinking about this. I felt vaguely that if the old woman would just go on shaking her contraption, a shiny white treasure would surely emerge from it. Perhaps she hadn't really gone so bankrupt that she couldn't even buy sugar. Maybe she had deliberately chosen not to use sugar. Otherwise, why would she have knocked the sugar jar I gave her to the ground?

=====

One day, after I had helped my family fetch water, I came here. She looked like a fossil sitting motionless on a wooden stool. This was a rare sight. It was drizzling, and she was drenched. In the past, she would move her contraption under the tea shop's awning as soon as it began raining. I felt nervous. What on earth had happened? Could she have died? I moved closer to get a better look at her face.

"No matter how much energy you put into your work, the hungry ghosts will eat everything you make."

She said this abruptly, but even her mouth was motionless. How had she spoken? Maybe these words were just the thoughts in her head and I could actually hear her thoughts.

The contraption was already thick with rust, and a hole had rusted out in the sheet iron. Scared stiff, I shook the rusted crank. Suddenly, that crank made a frightening vibrating sound, and my mind went blank. I fell down on the ground. I tried hard to remember, but I had no idea what that sound was. It felt as if I'd been shut up in a secret metal room and someone had hammered on a piece of armored plate. No, this sound was even worse: it could make a person lose his mind.

It took a long, long time for me to recover. When I looked up, the old woman had disappeared. Under the contraption was a large ball of multi-colored cotton candy. A dirty hand grabbed it right away and took off. The owner of the hand was the little girl Amei—that sick little kid. She ate it as she ran off. In the blink of an eye, the cotton candy dissolved in her mouth. When I caught up and seized hold of her, she opened her big mouth and started crying.

"Shake out one just like it and give it to me!" I ordered.

Whimpering, Amei nervously went back to the contraption. She was short, so it was only by standing on tiptoe that she could reach the crank. I stopped up my ears with my fingers.

The strange thing was that Amei wasn't the least bit afraid of the sound that the contraption made. She kept shaking it as hard as she could. Perspiration beaded her face. When she stopped, however, no cotton candy appeared. Standing on the small bench and manipulating this contraption, Amei was the picture of health—as if she weren't sick at all. She was like a little hero—arms akimbo—looking at me.

I peered under the contraption and saw that a few gears and screws had fallen off. I concluded that this contraption was ruined, so I paid no more attention to Amei. I lazily dragged myself home. Dad was at the front door scolding me, for I was supposed to be helping carry the groceries.

———

It was a long time before I could figure out what had happened. I kept seeing the old woman sitting, unmoving, in front of a pile of rags. If I approached her, a sound came out of her chest. By fits and starts, that sound sometimes spoke of her past glory, and sometimes it was only a string of curses. Once, I smelled an odor on her body. Startled, I felt her forehead. She lifted her eyelids to look at me. Her strange gaze frightened me. In the deep recesses of my dark memories a lot of little jars were being opened, and floating in the air was the fragrant scent of honey. I opened my mouth and said an irrelevant word: "Chasing." The word interrupted my memories. Just then, the old woman's gaze fell away, and she didn't look at me again.

I saw Little Zheng and the others take the gears from beneath the contraption. They said they could make tops to play with. And so one day, in the strong sunlight, we played with the tops until perspiration ran off us like rain. But even this exciting game couldn't satisfy me. In the evening, we grew tired of playing with the gears and threw them into the river. "This is boring! This is boring!" Little Zheng and Little Ying were wailing. I suggested that we visit the old woman. But when we arrived, she wasn't there. Only then did I remember that every time I'd seen her, I'd been alone. When I asked Little Zheng if he had seen the old woman, he was baffled. He said they hadn't seen her for a long time. They didn't believe that the old woman could sit on a pile of scrap iron every day. They said something must be wrong with my eyes. Long after Little Zheng and the others had left, I stood there examining the scrap iron. I even considered appropriating it and taking it home. Naturally, I didn't dare; if I did, Father would kill me.

The next day, the old woman was sitting there again.

"Hey, Little Qing. Hey, Little Qing. You're out of your mind," Amei taunted me.

I thought the children were all on to me: they must be jealous of my desire to become a vendor. Somebody might secretly sabotage my plan. But where could I raise the money? I had to force the old woman to divulge her secret recipe for shaking cotton candy out of thin air. I also had to ask her how to get rid of the strange, frightening sound that the contraption made. If it weren't for that sound, wouldn't I have already shaken out lots of multi-colored cotton candy?

Ah, she beckoned to me! From a long way away, I saw her beckoning to me! After setting down my dinner bowl, I ran toward her, even though Mother was scolding me from behind. I ran over to the old woman. How strange. She'd reverted to the way she was before: she was like a fossil, motionless.

"Granny—quick! Please teach me your secret recipe."

I said this three times in a row.

She pointed at the contraption. I looked, but it was no longer there. There were only some flies licking the syrup that had fallen to the ground. The old woman stood up, pretending to turn the crank. I heard the tremendous sound again. After shaking it for a while, she looked disheartened and sat down heavily on the wooden stool. She uttered a crisp sound from her mouth, but not from her throat: "Take it!" I looked at the ground: nothing was there.

My hopes had been dashed: How could I reconcile myself to this? For so many years, my only goal had been to be a vendor—one like this trickster. Not only did I want to shake cotton candy out of thin air, but I also wanted to shake out little golden bells. First, I had to amass capital and buy a contraption and practice. But I had no capital. With no capital, I had to shake a treasure out of thin air that could turn into money for real. The old woman was my only hope. With my own eyes, I'd seen her empty hands shake out cotton candy. I couldn't let this hope be dashed. As I reasoned with myself, I came up with a bizarre, audacious plan.

That morning, while the adults were at work at the bamboo-ware factory, Little Zheng and I began putting our plan to kidnap the old woman into effect. Everything went smoothly: we didn't even need our rope and chair, because the old woman made no sound as we manipulated her. Little Zheng and I carried her, letting her old legs drag on the ground. She was heavy. After we dragged her to the custodian's tool shed, we were ready to pass out from exhaustion. When we flung her to the ground, we also fell down and couldn't get up for a long time.

"Let's starve her and see if she opens her mouth or not!" Little Zheng said angrily.

We knew that she had only an alcoholic son at home, so there would be no problem for a while.

When we glanced at her, we saw that she was coiled into a ball on the ground. She was pawing at the dust with one hand and rubbing her face with it. Her face was now as black as the bottom of a pot, and her crocodile-like eyeballs were turning slowly. Little Zheng and I felt uneasy: Could she have some sinister motive?

"Granny, do you want something to eat?"

I had no sooner said this when my eyes were blurred by dust; they hurt too much to open. The old woman had thrown a handful of dust—accurately and ruthlessly. I had never expected this. I heard Little Zheng kick the old woman.

"Water! Water!" I shouted wildly.

<hr />

In unbearable pain, I had no recollection of how Little Zheng got me home. The next day, my eyelids were swollen. Although I couldn't go out, I was still thinking about the tool shed. How was she getting along there? I had a hard time waiting until afternoon when my parents left. Then I got out of bed. Covering my eyes with a washcloth, I moved to the door. From outside came the sound of running footsteps. Someone came in.

"Little Qing, little Qing, the floor of the tool shed is heaped with cotton candy. She's almost buried in it!" It was Little Zheng.

"Really? Really?"

"Alas, we were really dumb. Why didn't we wait and watch her sorcery?"

"She wouldn't let us."

"It's too bad that all of the sugar is filthy. Otherwise, we could sell it for a lot of money. The custodian swept it all into the garbage can. What a shame."

When Little Zheng and I finally went over there, we saw the

door of the tool shed standing open. She was sitting on top of a pile of brooms. I kept wiping my eyes with the washcloth. I despised this old woman. I heard a bunch of children coming this way: after a while, they formed a long line at the door.

"Here you go!" the old woman said to the little boy at the head of the line.

The little boy was holding the air with both hands; he went out rapturously.

"Here you go!" the old woman said to the second child—a little girl—in line.

The little girl was also holding the air with both hands; she, too, went out rapturously.

Like the head of a household, the old woman sat smugly on the brooms. Little Zheng and I were dumbfounded. Some of these children were from our neighborhood, others from elsewhere. What were they doing together with the old woman? Each child took ten or twenty cents from his pocket and gave it to her. The money was all real. After taking the money, she carefully put it into a pocket in the front of her garment. Soon, the pocket was bulging. When I looked outside, I was startled: I couldn't see the end of the long line. The custodians didn't mind postponing their work. They were looking on with interest, as if they were celebrating a holiday.

Little Zheng was seized by a whim: he also joined the line and waited. When it was his turn, the old woman—without even lifting her eyes—said, "Get out of here."

Little Zheng wasn't willing to move out of the way, and the other children angrily set upon him and threw him to the ground. He was like a drowned mouse. I helped him up, and in the midst of hisses from the other children, we left.

We went back to my home, where I lay down on the bed. I was still plagued by the same question: How could I amass enough capital to become a vendor? Sitting next to the bed, Little Zheng brainstormed: we could rob the old woman; in any case, she had earned her money fraudulently. I vetoed that idea. Unconvinced, he said, "She got the money through fraud."

I didn't think the old woman had been cheating people. I'd seen the multi-colored cotton candy, and I'd seen Amei eat it. The children's excited expressions had persuaded me that something I hadn't seen was real. I couldn't rob her. And it was useless to kidnap her. So how would I get the capital?

"What if we establish good relations with the other children, and make them do as we say and hand money over to us?" Little Zheng was talking nonsense.

In reality, the children not only wouldn't listen to us, but they had thrown Little Zheng down on the ground. Maybe the key was to gain their trust and then do what we wanted. For years, the old woman had shaken so much cotton candy out of that contraption that everyone believed she was a cotton candy vendor. Later, she used neither machinery nor sugar. Yet, everyone was still accustomed to the notion that she was a vendor. She had practiced this for years and years. We were just little kids; it was evident that no one would trust us. Even if we did trick people, no one would take the bait. We gave it a lot of thought. We couldn't figure out what to do, and yet we weren't willing to give up.

Someone came in. I thought it was my parents, and so I lay there very still. Little Zheng left the room to take a look. When he returned, his face was flushed. He poked me, meaning that I should get up right away.

I looked: the old woman was sitting in the outbuilding.

When Little Zheng and I walked over to her, she held out her hands. Each of us took hold of one hand and stood there waiting for her to speak.

"You can't cheat people," she said with her shriveled mouth.

Little Zheng and I nodded our heads earnestly.

We thought she wanted to say something else, but she seemed

tired of talking. She just lowered her eyes again and started snoozing. We were still holding her hands. I was afraid my parents would return and question us, so I had to urge her to leave my home. As soon as I made this clear, she opened her eyes and angrily called me "fickle."

Then my parents came back. They looked at the old woman sitting at the table, but said nothing. Weary of hanging around, Little Zheng went home.

When it was time for dinner, the old woman ate with us. My parents didn't seem to think this was unusual; it was as if the old woman were part of our family, not the vendor from two streets away. After eating, she rose to leave. When she reached the door, she suddenly turned around and said to me: "Every day, I sleep and dream amidst the cotton candy."

As she spoke, her breath and body both smelled sour. When I watched her walk into the distance, I was still tasting her words. Right up until Mother called me.

"You finally have some ambition. We feel reassured," Mama said.

This time, Father broke precedent and didn't scold me; rather, he stared at me questioningly for a long time.

The next day was another bright, sunny day. After I fetched water and dried vegetables, I walked over there. From a distance, I saw a long line of children, but the old woman wasn't at the head of the line. I saw Little Zheng again; he was sitting where the old woman used to sit. He and the children were exchanging knowing looks. He beckoned to me, and I sat side by side with him on the bench. One by one, the children came and solemnly smacked our palms. Although they didn't give us money, I felt utterly content. Little Zheng, the children, and I were immersed in daydreams about the multi-colored cotton candy. One after another, the honey jars in the depths of our memories were opened up: the strong fragrance overflowed into the air.

Mei lived on a small, lonely side street in the downtown area. The five-story building had been constructed in the 1950s. Mei and her husband Jin lived in a three-room apartment on the first floor.

Mei's home was a little unusual: except for the kitchen, all the appliances and furniture were covered with cloths of various colors, as if the two of them were about to go traveling. It was only when they wanted to use these things that they uncovered them. For example, at mealtimes, they removed the heavy tablecloth, and when they drank tea, they uncovered the tea table and sofa. Even the two large mirrors hanging on the walls were covered with embroidered cloths. Only when they looked in the mirrors did they uncover them. Because of these cloths, the rhythm of Mei's daily life was much slower than that of ordinary persons.

Mr. Jin seldom took off these covers, for Mei handled everything for him. All day long, he lay on a chaise lounge—the only piece of furniture that wasn't covered with a cloth—and read a thick book, *A Collection of Illustrations of Wild Plants*, and looked repeatedly at the pictures in it. Lying on the chaise lounge, he was staring with his left eye at the book's illustrations of *humid euphorbia* while at the same time glancing sideways at the shoe rack. He said loudly, "The cat has pulled the cloth on the shoe rack down to the floor!" From the kitchen, Mei heard him and rushed over to re-cover the shoe rack. Jin was obviously a sensitive person, too.

In the small garden outside, Mei grew neither flowers nor trees. From strips of bamboo and plastic film, she created an awning—a long one which looked ridiculous. Inside the plastic awning, she raised a strange plant from seeds that Jin had bought through a relative who lived in another place. The seeds were a small, purple crescent shape. Jin dug a furrow one foot deep and buried these seeds in it. He told Mei that this plant was the rare "underground plant." None of it was on the surface. After the seeds were buried, they would grow straight down. He also fertilized and watered their plants, and then Mei covered them with the plastic awning. Jin said, *After this, you don't need to tend them. You only need to keep this plastic awning in shape, that's all. When this plant grows underground, it makes strict demands of the environmental conditions. In short, the less environmental change the better.*

"Mei, what kind of treasure are you growing?" the neighbor Ayi asked.

"The China rose."

"Why don't I see any buds?"

"They grow downward, and the flowers also blossom underground. It isn't the China rose that we're accustomed to seeing. The flowers are only as large as grains of rice, and the petals are stiff."

Mei blushed. She was repeating what Jin had told her. In her own mind, she didn't have a good grasp of it. With her goldfish eyes bulging, Ayi looked at her for a moment and then silently entered the apartment.

Mei told Jin that their neighbor Ayi didn't believe they were growing the China rose. Jin was shaving just then, and lather covered his face. Blinking his little triangular eyes, he said he hadn't believed it either, at first. Whether people believe it or not has no bearing on the China rose's growth. With that, he went into the bathroom. Holding a mop, Mei stood there thinking. Presumably, Jin had a clear understanding of this. When the seeds were seen under lamplight, they did look like a singular variety. She remembered that two nights ago the two of them had put their heads together and taken stock of these seeds. She bent over and mopped the floor. When she reached the desk, she noticed a seed that had been left next to a leg of the desk. She quietly picked it up, wrapped it in crepe paper, and put it in the kitchen cupboard.

In the afternoon, Jin napped on the chaise lounge. As for Mei, she sat on the sofa. She could rest just by leaning against the back of the sofa and dozing a little. When her eyelids grew heavy, she heard someone knocking on the door. Twice. Not continuously, but with an interval between them. Who would knock this way? Was it a child playing a prank? She didn't open the door. She heard Jin snoring softly. After a while, just as her eyelids were growing heavy again, the knock came again—this time, twice in a row. Still light and hesitant. Mei had no choice but to go to the door.

Ayi was standing outside. Her face was pale, as if she'd been frightened.

"I'd also like to grow a little of that variety—that variety of China rose. Do you have any extra seeds?"

"No. Old Jin brought them back through a relative. If you want some, we can ask someone's help again."

Ayi looked terribly disappointed. Then her expression changed to spiteful probing—she impertinently stuck her head in and looked into the room. Mei generally did not invite neighbors into her home. Ayi's unusual behavior made her a little nervous.

"I just remembered. I still have one seed. Do you want it?" She looked almost ingratiating.

"You have one? Sure, I'd like it. Let me have it."

Taking the seed wrapped in crepe paper, Ayi gave Mei a hard look.

When Mei turned around to close the door, what she saw in the room startled her: a rat was sneaking back and forth under the tablecloth on the dining table. There had seldom been rats in their home. Was it really a rat? Pouncing, she covered the tablecloth with her hands, but the little guy still slipped away. She had pounced on air. She looked on helplessly as the gray rat climbed up the window and glided outside. Shaken, Mei stood in the room and said, "Rat."

Jin's gaze left his book, and he glanced at her. Then he returned to the book and said:

"The rat is Ayi. You needn't worry too much."

Recovering, she replaced the tablecloth and went to the kitchen. After cooking for a while, she rushed back to the bedroom because she was afraid of the rat. Luckily, she didn't see the little guy again. But she noticed that the lower part of the cloth on the dresser had been gnawed on, so it seemed this problem was real! When Mei was in primary school, the city was overrun with rats. People had employed all kinds of ways to get rid of them: blocking their paths, poisoning, tracking, pouring water on their nests, and so on. From then on, there had been no problem.

As she chopped radishes, she savored what Jin had said. Jin had said the rat was simply Ayi. This made some sense. Although the two families were next-door neighbors, and their children had played together, their socializing had been limited to simple greetings made in passing after the children grew up and moved away. So she'd been a little surprised when Ayi had asked for flower seeds. Judging by Ayi's expression and movements, she was taking this matter quite seriously. But why? It couldn't be merely for a few flower seeds.

At mealtime, Mei said to her husband:

"Will Ayi really grow the seed she took with her? What do you think?"

"No, because that one is fake; it's one I culled to throw away. Altogether, quite a few are fake. As soon as she looks at it, she'll realize that. It isn't a flower seed; it's a beautiful pebble."

Jin winked at her complacently. Mei whispered to herself: "You cunning bastard!" She was a little worried that Ayi would hold a grudge against her because of this. Ayi's husband was a sullen, one-eyed man. Would the couple think she had played a trick on them? Perhaps she should explain to them. Jin argued against this. He said it would be a case of "confusing the issue with more talk." He also said, "Since she's interested in this underground plant, it's okay to make fun of her a little."

———

Because of insomnia, Mei and Jin had started sleeping in separate rooms ten years earlier. In general, Mei could sleep from midnight to a little after one o'clock. After awakening, she couldn't sleep again until after three o'clock. She would wake up again about five o'clock, and at close to seven o'clock she slept again for a while. She arose at sometime after eight o'clock. Every day was much like this. Mei's nights were long. At first, this was hard to put up with. Between periods of sleep, she was drowsy. After awakening at one o'clock at night, dressed in her pajamas, she always made the rounds of each room. While doing this, she didn't turn on any lights. And so, one night she fell—frightened of the sudden glare on the large mirror in the living room—and bumped against the side of the dining table. She broke her collarbone. Looking back on it, she thought the subtle sparkle had been caused by a passing car. Afterward, Mei had covered everything with cloths. After getting better, Mei ceased her nighttime rounds. She still got up during the night and sat on a low kitchen stool. Leaning against the wall, she would doze for a while. She sat in the kitchen because she could look out the window and see the sky and the trees. This was relaxing. At such times, recalling the long-ago days when she and her children had been together, she was astonished at the well-being she felt: Was that really the life she had experienced? The sense of well-being, however, came from her present contentment. Thus, after a long time, she started enjoying her insomnia. She imagined that she had become a large white goose waddling in the woods looking for food.

Unless he was greatly disturbed—for example, the time that Mei was injured—Jin did not wake up at night. According to him, he slept lightly: whenever something happened, he was aware of it.

"People like me are bound to die early, because we never have any real peace."

He made a long face when he spoke of his situation, but Mei knew he was inwardly satisfied. Wasn't light sleep much the same as wakefulness? If a person was always waking up, wasn't this the same as living two lifetimes? Jin's lifetime had been a really good bargain! What's more, he was so healthy that he never fell ill: How could he die prematurely? He also said that he had never dreamed, because he was essentially always conscious and so there was no way to dream. As Mei listened, she thought: When she sat in the kitchen and dozed, she had one dream after another. The two of them were really not much alike.

Jin supported Mei in covering the furniture and other articles, because he also hated the glare from these things at night. "Even though I do sleep, now and then I open my eyes and see that eerie scene."

The city had more and more cars, and people's night life lasted longer and longer, and so cars had recently been passing Mei's home all night long. After the furniture and other articles were covered, Mei felt that her home was "as solid as a huge rock." The lamplight that swept past from the cars looked fleeting and insubstantial, and could no longer scare her. Jin was happy, too. He kept saying, "This is great, just great." He added that although he didn't wake up at night, he was quite aware of the cars' rudeness.

"People call this herb 'snakehead king.' It can cure snakebites. In the past, it grew all over outside our old home. There were also numerous snakes there. This is the law of combating poison with poison."

Jin placed the book on his chest, closed his eyes, and lay there. Mei saw only that his mouth was moving. Amused by this, she couldn't help but interrupt:

"The herb's scientific name is '*yizhi huanghua*!'"

"Oh, you know this, too. When did you read my book?!"

"At night. My eyesight keeps improving. I can read by the faint light that comes through the windows from the street lamps."

A slight smile floated up on Jin's face. Mei wondered how far down the China rose had grown. Maybe Jin should have studied botany when he was young, but instead he had been a salesman. But if Jin had really become a botanist, could he have lived the kind of life he had now? Would the room be filled with plant specimens hanging everywhere? In recent years, he had read this same book about wild plants every day; he had never collected specimens. Not long before, Jin, who seldom went out, had rushed to the city center and brought back these China rose seeds. He had vaguely mentioned a relative's name, so it seemed that this person had sent them to him.

Mei read Jin's book in order to search for clues to Jin's thinking. She admired him greatly. He was so calm! Even though a rat had sneaked into their home, he wasn't fazed. By contrast, Mei had gone through a period of despair after breaking her collarbone. Along with an aunt who came to help out, Jin silently took responsibility for some of the housework. He seldom consoled her. Perhaps this was because of Jin's composure. Mei recovered through struggling by herself. As soon as she regained her strength, Jin lay down on his chaise lounge again. He said with a smile that he was "about the same as a paralyzed person." Mei thought his smile was one of contentment.

The accumulation of water in front of the door was something that happened all of a sudden. It had rained for two days and two nights, and mud had clogged the sewer. By midnight, the front of the apartment had turned into a pool. Just then, Jin had jumped out of bed and rushed barefoot into the rain. The battery-powered light on the windowsill was shining on the plastic awning over the flowers. Wielding a hoe, he worked hard in the rain. After about two hours, he had dug a trench to divert the accumulated water. It had never occurred to Mei that Jin could still be so energetic. It was as though he were fighting for his life.

When he returned, he was too tired to talk. He slowly removed his wet raincoat and slowly lay back down. Mei rubbed his hair with a dry towel.

"The flowers are safe now. They'd all be dead if I hadn't saved them. We can't imagine what the growing environment underground is like. We can only infer what it is. I learned about this once . . ."

With that, he went to sleep. As he snored, his lips moved slightly. Mei wondered what he was saying. Was he talking with the underground plants?

In the morning, the sun came out. Standing at the plastic-film awning, Ayi was looking around suspiciously.

"Mei, nothing is growing in here. Could we dismantle the awning? They're interfering with the drain, and they don't look good, either."

"Ayi, how can you say this? I planted them myself. I told you they're the China rose, a special variety that grows underground. During the night, Jin brought them back from the brink of death."

"Huh. You're really stubborn and deluded. Some people are still really pleased to live this way."

Ayi's husband called out to her from their home. When she went home, she turned around again and looked at the flowerbed a few times. Mei thought her expression was filled with curiosity; that's to say that Ayi certainly wasn't convinced of what she had said. Then, she heard Ayi and her husband arguing in loud voices. What they were arguing about, however, she couldn't hear.

When Mei entered the apartment, she saw that Jin was still sleeping. He was so calm. Suddenly, Mei wondered: What if all the flower seeds they had planted were beautiful little pebbles? She thought back for a while: it seemed this was really possible. When she had held them in her hand, they had felt cold and had also made a *ding ding* sound! Was it because of this quality that they could grow downward and blossom? Ayi had evidently mis-understood. If you believed in something like this, it was true; if you didn't believe in it, it wasn't. Ayi evidently didn't believe in it.

More than thirty years ago, when the newly married Mei and the newly married Ayi had moved to this building, it was desolate here. Mei frequently noticed her neighbor take a small stool out-side and sit at the entrance to watch the setting sun. When, little by little, the last rays turned dark, the view of this woman's back gave her a sense not only of loneliness but also of stubbornness. When they saw each other, they were courteous, as were the two husbands. Mei seldom saw Ayi's husband. He was a steelworker, and he always stayed inside after work. A gloomy atmosphere hung over their home. Mei thought that Ayi and her husband were well suited; they never quarreled. Then what were they arguing about today? The flower seeds? Now the setting sun couldn't be seen. Life went on indoors, but the view of her back in the past had lasted until today. In the past, when the setting sun could be seen, the future was still hidden entirely in confusion.

━━━

"My relative lives at No. 3 Youma Lane. It's a distant relative, so we ordinarily don't see one another. If you're interested, you can go to see him. Because that place has undergone reconstruction, it's a little hard to find."

Jin was speaking of the relative who had given him the flower seeds.

"If I go to see him, I'll have to find an excuse," Mei said.

"You can ask him how to grow the brilliant purple China rose."

Mei was excited. After eating lunch, she skipped her nap, tidied up a little, and went out.

In the clusters of new construction in the city center, Youma Lane had disappeared. Mei asked several persons before learning that the old building at No. 3 Youma Lane had been demolished, and all the former residents had been resettled in a row of simple single-story houses. An old tire repairman told her that Teacher Bing now lived in the westernmost building.

At first, Mei was startled by Teacher Bing's appearance. He was like a wild man: a mass of gray whiskers covered his face, and gray hair fell below his shoulders. He was bleary-eyed.

"Ah, the brilliant purple China rose." His voice buzzed out from his whiskers. "This is a variety that used to exist, but now no one can grow it successfully. The rules for growing it are simple: it grows only when you forget it."

"How does one forget it?"

"Each person has his own ways. For example, I scatter seeds everywhere at random—next to the ditch, in holes people dig for trees, in the holes of new house foundations, in the earth on old thatched roofs, and so forth. One day, I saw a bulge in the earthen wall of a thatched hut. After I moved the mud on it, my plant was revealed. After thinking about it, I finally remembered that I had sown seeds on top of the wall. Mei, it's better if you don't look into this too much."

As he talked, Teacher Bing was frowning, as if displeased by her presence—and also as if he were disclosing his secret only because he had no alternative. But still, he told Mei that this bungalow where he lived was originally No. 3 Youma Lane.

"The ground beneath this land is overgrown with many varieties of flowers: it's like floral fossils. People who live here are all old hands at this. I've heard that the foundations of the high new buildings are very deep. That doesn't matter. Our plants have all vanished from the surface of the earth, as if they had never existed . . ."

After leaving the relative's home, Mei walked two or three minutes in confusion and then lost her way. She wanted to ask directions, but there was no one to ask: she could see only the remains of demolished houses. In the blink of an eye, the city had disappeared.

"Teacher Bing!!" she shouted.

The caw of a crow answered her—there were still crows here, calling to mind the former city.

"Jin!!" she shouted.

Jin appeared on the distant horizon and, carrying a wooden bucket in one hand, he slowly approached her. Breathing heavily, he placed the wooden bucket on the ground. The water sloshed out.

"What kind of fish are these?" Mei asked.

"Deep-water fish. The pile-driver over there startled them, and they mistakenly scurried up. River water isn't suitable for these creatures. I want to free them. Why don't you go home first?"

Carrying the bucket, Jin walked far away. At first, Mei considered catching up with him and then gave up this idea, because she could see the city once again. Teacher Bing's house was just ahead, wasn't it? She entered that side street and reached the main street. She thought to herself: In the past, could Jin also have lived in Youma Lane? And Ayi, too?

At night, Mei saw dazzling light swaying again on the portiere. It was a strange sight. Later, light appeared on all of the furniture's cloth covers: now and then, the interior of the apartment turned brilliant. The stream of cars on the road was unceasing. Mei thought all her efforts had been in vain. Sometimes, ill-mannered drivers would blow their horns. When the horns suddenly sounded, Mei sometimes would instantly lose consciousness.

Breaking with precedent, Jin didn't sleep that night. He said, "Those deep-water fish get on everyone's nerves." Lying on the chair, he kept sighing and called the phenomena that had manifested themselves in the daytime "perverse."

"Actually, I acted unnecessarily. They all died. See, an ordinary person like me can't see their purpose. Their existence in and of itself scares people, doesn't it? Listen!!"

Mei saw that the right side of Jin's face was alight. The sound of the cars' horns was tumultuous.

He stood up and walked around, greatly stimulated. Mei saw that the light was following him constantly. For a second, the light stopped at his eyes, and his eyes then turned green and strange-shaped. Mei shouted from fright and lost consciousness again.

After Mei came to, she heard *dili, dili.* It was Jin fiddling with the flower seeds. It was a little warm in the room because he had drawn the thick drapes. All the lights were out except for a small reading lamp on the desk. All of a sudden, Mei felt as if she were living in a cave. She groped her way toward the study.

"Have a seat," Jin said, pointing to a chair beside him. "This is something I asked Teacher Bing for today."

Ah, it wasn't flower seeds. It was a beautiful gem.

"He no longer has anywhere to plant seeds. He gave it to me. I was really baffled."

In the lamplight, Mei picked up a jade-green seed, and the light immediately penetrated it. She noticed a dark little spot floating inside it. She couldn't keep from saying:

"These are all stones; they aren't plants."

"Hmm. Could be. Anything is possible, isn't it?"

In the lamplight, Jin's eyeballs became two blank dots. He turned around.

Mei took stock of his back, which reminded her of how he looked when he appeared on the horizon of the ruins today. She heard two people digging outside. It must be Ayi and her husband.

"I gave them seeds," Jin said without moving.

Mei wanted to get up and go outside, but Jin checked her, saying:

"Don't look. It's something private—just between them."

RAINSCAPE

I like to sit at the desk and tally the accounts. I look out the window: a gray structure built of granite is about one hundred meters away. Its windows—two rows of them—are all positioned in high places. Each window is narrow, and at night most of them are dark. A little faint light shines through from only two or three windows, giving people an unfathomable feeling. In front of the structure is a path, where people in twos or threes frequently pass by. Some are going to work, some are running errands, and some are children going to school. They all walk quite rapidly. In the sunlight, their shadows flash past the stone wall. I've never seen anyone emerge from the granite building, whose small black iron front door has been closed for years. But on the door is a large, new, gold-colored lock.

One day, when I was at the desk and facing the window in a daze, my husband said from behind me, "Listen. Someone in back is weeping."

Terrified, I concentrated intently, but neither heard nor saw anything. Out in front, because there had just been a rainstorm and there was still the sound of light rain, no one was on the path. But the granite building was actually a little different.

"Someone's coming over," my husband said. "It's the person who was weeping."

I held my breath and waited. I waited a long time. There was no one. The rain fell heavily again, with a *hualala* sound. The shrubbery was bending in the wind. My face fell, and I said, "Why don't I see anyone?"

"What a shame. I think it's your brother. With a flash of bright light, he disappeared on the wall. I wish you had seen this." My husband was still emotionally absorbed in what was happening.

"Did he completely vanish on the wall?"

"I certainly heard him weeping—over there, next to the persimmon tree."

The week before, Brother had come to our home. He hadn't been well-dressed and looked like a tramp. But he didn't talk at all the way a tramp does. He's always been shy, saying very little. Each time he comes to our home, he sits in a corner, for he doesn't want to attract any attention. Because he doesn't have a real job, my husband feels guilty and gives him a little money now and then. Brother takes the money and sneaks away. It's always a long time before he shows up again.

When talking about him, my parents say, "We don't know what to think of him. We never get a clear-cut impression of him."

Could what happened be a figment of my husband's imagination? I wanted to ask him, but he had already forgotten the incident. He had picked up the account books and was examining them carefully.

People were passing by in front of the granite wall—two young people, a man and a girl. The girl was lame. Holding aloft a large, sky-blue umbrella, the man was keeping the woman from being drenched by the rain. They were talking as they walked. A long time passed before I could hear their alternately loud and soft voices. Blending with the sound of the rain, their voices remained out there below the gray sky.

After a few days, Brother came over and sat on the edge of the desk, dangling his skinny legs. When I mentioned the granite structure across the way, his face immediately clouded over.

"I always hear someone weeping there," I said.

"Why don't you walk over to the front of the wall and take a careful look?" Brother mumbled as he jumped down from the desk. With his back to the window, he blocked my line of sight. "Fantasy is still the way we do things best."

Lowering his head, he walked out, seemingly quite irritated.

The granite façade glimmered in the murky twilight. Next to the wall, some people walking past were dimly visible. What on earth was going on over there? I hadn't heard Brother weeping; I had just wanted to draw him out to talk about some things, and so I had lied to him. He must have grown angry because he saw through my ruse. Could my husband have told a lie? I made up my mind to go over to the wall the next day to take a close look.

———

It could be said that I had "turned a blind eye" to this building for years. The granite wall was very old with dark watermarks on it. This was a deserted building. I heard a key turn twice in the lock, and the door opened with a creak. I went inside without a second thought.

A person with his back to me was standing in the empty corridor. In the dim light, I couldn't get a good look at his face. I thought he was crying.

"On the 18th of April, you saw the beginning and the end of the matter," he said, his bare head gleaming and closing in on me. I still couldn't see his face well. I waited for him to go on talking, but he didn't: it was as if something had struck him. Bending over, he began to sob softly.

No one else was in the corridor, and the atmosphere was gloomy. He squatted against the wall and cried. As he sobbed, his aged back shuddered. Just then, from somewhere outside, I heard the sound of a car rolling by. At the end of the corridor, someone quite angrily bumped into the door with a *peng*.

"Probably you know my brother?" I bent down and shouted at the man.

"It's too late. Too late!" he said, out of breath, through his tears.

As I stood there, both ashamed and afraid, countless emotions welled up in my heart. He began scrabbling at the crumbly limestone wall with his fingers, making a nerve-racking sound. The dust kept falling.

"Brother! Brother! Don't leave me behind alone!" I blurted out in despair.

At this, the person stopped crying right away and stood up like a gravely wounded wild animal. He turned toward me. Now he and I were so close to one another that we couldn't have been any closer. His sleeves touched my hand. The strange thing was that his face was still a dark shadow. No matter which angle I looked from, I couldn't see his true face. It was as if the light couldn't reach it.

He began backing away from me. For each of his steps backward, I took a step forward. Our entangled shadows were reflected on the wall; it looked as if we were fighting. I felt an unparalleled tension. All of a sudden, the doors on both sides of the corridor opened, and he turned around and fled. It seemed that people in all the rooms were craning their necks to watch. I didn't dare stay here, so I turned, too, and ran out the front door.

I stopped at the end of the path. Looking back, I saw that the door was still standing wide open. Inside, the corridor was pitch-dark, and the lights in those few windows had all been turned off. The structure had once more become lifeless. I looked up at the sky: it was actually already daybreak.

People were coming around from the path over there, talking in low voices. I saw the lame girl and the young man again. Although it wasn't raining, the young man was still holding a large, sky-blue umbrella aloft. When they passed me, the two of them were dumbfounded for a moment and stopped walking.

Lowering my head, I rushed forward. I didn't dare look at them. After walking quite far, in the end I couldn't keep from looking back. They were still standing in the same place, and in the first rays of morning sun, the large blue umbrella glittered with light. The man was bending his head to say something to the girl. Behind them, the granite wall of the lifeless building was blurry and remote.

When I got home, my husband was already up. He was sitting there neatly dressed, as if he was intending to go out. He set my breakfast on the table.

"Time flew last night. I overslept," he said.

It was strange: he had the same feeling. Was time different inside and outside the building? As I drank some milk, I peeped at his face. When they were dreaming, could people tell any difference in time? Since he had slept straight through, how did he know whether time had passed quickly or slowly?

"What's the 18th of April?"

"It's the anniversary of your older brother's death. Have you forgotten even this?" He was a little surprised.

"At night, people can forget anything, no matter what it is."

"True. I've felt this, too. In one short night, innumerable things can occur."

I walked over to the desk, and my gaze settled on that wall. The room suddenly felt sultry. Like a small fish, a faint desire swam back and forth. My husband went out, heading in the opposite direction from that building. He kept hesitating, as if he were thinking of backtracking to take a look and then giving up the idea. Turning a corner, he disappeared. The leaves on the date tree at the doorway were moist. Had someone sprayed it with insecticide, or had it rained hard again during the night? Brother had told me last time that he would leave here soon. This was the first time in his life that he was going far away. I asked where he was going. He replied laconically, "I'll just keep going."

When he said this, I recalled my husband's description of him a couple of days ago. When a person disappears like a ray of light into the wall, what does time mean to him? Our parents' faces were alight with joy, their dispositions softening at once. Because of their tardy expression of love for my brother, they both felt a little confused and said they regretted being unable to accompany their son on his journey. If they had been ten years younger, they could have.

When he left, he kept looking back, his face darkening, his appearance dejected. When he was about to get into the car, Mother hung on to the strap of his backpack and wouldn't let go. When the car started up, Father followed, jumping along like a locust, thus giving rise to jokes from passersby. As soon as the car disappeared around a corner, the two old people sat down on the ground, looking demented. My husband and I had to exert ourselves to get them back into the house. They sat side by side on the couch, and Mother suddenly asked quietly: "How can someone who has everything going for him be carried away by a car?"

My husband tried his best to explain. He said my brother hadn't disappeared from this world: he was merely taking a trip. This was common enough in other families. He would enjoy himself for a while in the outside world and come back again before long.

Sneering at his explanation, Mother said, "Have the two of you reached an agreement with him? Your father and I are old. We passed our prime a long time ago. But even though we're old, we're still alert. We've also heard about what happened in front of your house: it's exactly what we predicted. When you chose to move down here, we talked about it."

Then she took Father's hand and looked at it carefully. After a while, the two of them dozed off.

———

I started seriously considering making an inspection behind the building. We hadn't gone there since we moved here more than ten years ago, because there was a craggy hill behind the granite wall. My husband and I always thought there was nothing worth looking at. Before falling asleep, I mentioned my plan to my husband. He said vaguely, "What if you get lost?"

Early in the morning, I set off in that direction. I had no sooner reached the path than I saw two people ahead of me: it was the lame girl and the tall youth. This time, they weren't carrying an umbrella. Empty-handed, they turned around and stood facing me. This time, I saw that the "girl" was actually a middle-aged person wearing a wig, and the "youth" was a thin old geezer who was almost seventy years old. They beckoned to me, asking me to approach them.

Impatient, I spoke first. "I see that the two of you always go over there. I've watched you from the window lots of times. What's it like there? I really want a complete concept of this building."

They laughed in unison. I didn't think their laughter was genuine, and I wondered all of a sudden if they were two ghosts, ghosts that had floated out from that deserted building. Frightened, I unconsciously recoiled, but I also kept staring at them.

A key turned in the lock. At the *ka-ta* sound, I fled for my life. After running a short distance, I stopped again and looked back: the two of them had disappeared. The door was wide open; inside was the corridor I was familiar with. They had probably gone inside. Thinking of the first impression I'd had of them and of the bright colorful umbrella, I felt my knees weaken. I didn't dare go behind the granite wall again: because of this episode, I'd lost the little confidence I'd had early in the morning.

I went back home, where my husband was sitting in my usual place. His head was bent as he repaired the alarm clock, and the desk was covered with parts and tools.

"You've been gone a long time. It's almost time for lunch," he said without raising his head.

"True. And I couldn't find a way to reach the back of the building."

I thought, annoyed, that perhaps he was also faking it. Sitting here, he had seen everything that transpired this morning. I shouldn't have retreated: I was really ashamed of myself. What was there to be afraid of? The two ghosts? They might have been nothing but two locksmiths or pharmacists when they were alive. After their deaths, they had disguised themselves. It was nothing more than that.

As I was reasoning like this, the alarm clock suddenly rang with an insistent and terrible sound. It went on and on, as if it would never stop, and it vibrated so much that it numbed my brain. When the sound finally stopped, my husband had disappeared, and nothing was on the desk. Yet, I had seen the desk covered with his tools. Was he sitting here and playing a trick on me? He said, "You've been gone *a long time.*" This was a hint.

I looked out the window. The door was closed, and a little light glimmered on the granite wall. At the upper left corner, close to the eaves, there seemed to be a ball of bright light. My heart throbbing, I wondered again what on earth it was like behind the building. I still had to find out; no one could stop me. Even if the two ghosts wanted to discourage me, they couldn't guard the path every minute, could they? They must be careless some of the time. A huge time difference existed between the inside of the structure and the outside of it. If they weren't ghosts and were just two ordinary people, how could they be accustomed to this time difference? My husband had confirmed the time difference: What if he was also lying?

Every day, I faced that gray granite wall, with my brother's situation lingering in my mind. He had left by car, but that was only a superficial phenomenon. This superficial impression remained in my parents' minds. The black iron door opened and then closed again, closed and then opened again: the lame woman and the tall youth walked out from there and opened the large sky-blue umbrella. Standing in the rain, they chattered incessantly. One time, I told my husband of the scene I had observed. My husband blinked and said quietly that he had just come in from outside and that it certainly was not raining. It was a bright spring day. He was contemplating hanging his laundry out to dry in the sun. Nonetheless, I still heard the sound of raindrops falling on the umbrella. One of the woman's sleeves was drenched on one side. It was really mystifying.

Mr. Yuanpu had really declined. When Jinglan entered that rundown home and the maid Yunma opened Yuanpu's bedroom door, he was sitting on a chamber pot, taking a crap, and thinking. Maybe he was merely pretending to think and actually was dozing. Looking closely at him, Jinglan confirmed this from his drooling. Since he'd last seen him, his color had grown much grayer. He seemed a little embarrassed, for he immediately wiped his ass, pulled up his pants, and stood up. The smell of shit filled the room at once. When he rapped on the table, Yunma came in and carried the chamber pot out, closing the door behind her and leaving the smell shut up inside. After he and Jinglan looked at each other in speechless despair, Yuanpu staggered toward the big bed, straightened the rumpled bedding, and then lay down and carefully covered his legs. From the way the bed looked, Jinglan knew that he had spent another sleepless night.

"Have you had breakfast?" Jinglan asked with concern.

"Sure I have. Otherwise, how would I be able to defecate?" He was mocking himself. There were thick mats on Yuanpu's bed. Jinglan estimated that there were five or six of them, each with cotton batting weighing about ten pounds. Yuanpu had three extremely large pillows. At the moment two pillows were behind his decrepit back, and the other leaned against the side of the bed next to the wall. Yuanpu was half-lying on this large pile of cotton batting, but his face was telegraphing agony, as though the soft cotton batting were rubbing and hurting his body. This old home was much higher than ordinary houses. Many years ago, when Jinglan was a child, there had once been a large window in the wall. A bamboo shade had hung from it. Now only a cursorily whitewashed windowpane remained. Yuanpu had taken this action because in recent years he had found windows increasingly repellant. There were no chairs in the room, so Jinglan sat on the night table at the head of the bed. When he had visited the year before, Yuanpu had told him to sit there. When Jinglan considered his friendship with Yuanpu, he couldn't help feeling proud of himself. But in recent years, Yuanpu's decrepitude made him a little uneasy. Yuanpu's sitting on the chamber pot was especially disgusting. Yuanpu had always been a sanitary person. You could even say he was fastidious. It hadn't occurred to Jinglan that he could change so much. He certainly wasn't so ill that he had to stay in bed. He was perfectly capable of getting up and going to the bathroom next door, but for the last six months, he had always asked Yunma to bring a chamber pot to his room. The stench was so bad that even Yunma held her nose when she entered and left the room. Jinglan thought, *When all is said and done, there comes a day when people go downhill*; even a sagacious thinker like his mentor would not be able to avoid declining day after day. Who could defy the laws of nature? In the past, Yuanpu had suffered only from insomnia, but ten years ago, this hadn't troubled him at all. Time after time, he and Jinglan had argued all night long in this room, and in the daytime, he was in his usual good spirits. When Jinglan tried to imagine what Yuanpu would look like in two or three years, he smiled sadly.

"Your color is really bad. You ought to exercise more in the courtyard. Exercise would give you a better appetite." Jinglan couldn't help saying this, but he soon wished he hadn't. Yuanpu leaned back on his pillow and listened attentively, but he wasn't listening to Jinglan: he was listening to the noise outside. When he pulled himself together, Jinglan thought that all traces of senility had vanished from his face. His eyes glittered with bright light. He looked like a young man—absolutely different from the way he had looked a moment ago.

"It's Yunma," he said in a low voice. "She's asked her fellow villagers to come here for meetings every night. If you had come at night, you would have seen the house ablaze with lamps. It's hilarious."

Jinglan was astonished. How could anything so preposterous have actually happened? Yunma was Yuanpu's old servant. Long ago, she had agreed to wait on him until the end. A servant had actually taken advantage of him. After he recovered from his astonishment, he felt melancholy again. It appeared that Yuanpu couldn't control his own life. Who could help him? How could someone with such self-esteem accept help from others?

"I don't mind. It gives me pleasure in my old age. You know that I wearied long ago of argument."

Jinglan wondered: *Could he be lying to cover up his embarrassment?* He also thought that he was certainly much different than he used to be. Jinglan glanced around the room: decades had passed, and yet this room was the same as always. The only difference was that it looked much gloomier and more rundown. A crab basket in the corner was covered with thick dust. In the old days, he and Yuanpu had gone crabbing in the mountain streams.

"I have to go. I'll come back another day. I'll be staying in town longer this time."

Yuanpu didn't respond. He was still listening intently to the activity outside. Jinglan waited a little longer. He was uneasy as he rose to leave: he thought his mentor had forgotten he was there.

As soon as he left the room, Yunma grabbed his arm and drew him to her room, which was across the hall from Yuanpu's. A lot of miscellaneous stuff was piled up all over: it seemed to be the old woman's hobby. Yunma stared at Jinglan. He was puzzled and so he took the initiative to find something to talk about. He brought up Yuanpu's present condition, hinting that Yunma should keep the house quiet: this was essential if the elderly Yuanpu were to spend his last years in tranquility. From what Yunma told Jinglan, Yuanpu's condition was worrisome: he was absolutely different from the way he was in the past. She had worked here more than thirty years: her service should have been appreciated. But for more than two years now, Yuanpu had been unusually strict with her. Her mother was more than eighty and needed care, so she had brought her here. This house had plenty of empty rooms, and she herself was in good health: she could take care of two elderly persons at once. She had settled her mother into a room upstairs. In the beginning, Yuanpu was happy about this, too. He went upstairs every day to chat with the old woman about household trivia. They were from the same generation and got along well. Her mother had a good impression of Yuanpu, too, saying that he was modest and unassuming, easy to be around. But before long, Yunma realized something was wrong. Yuanpu went upstairs too often—sometimes two or three times a day—and not about anything important, either. This made her mother uncomfortable. Yunma asked her mother if Yuanpu had suddenly started "looking for romance in his sunset years"? Her mother denied this. At first, she didn't want to talk about it. Later on, she said that what the old geezer was interested in was something else, for several times he had tried to goad her into betraying her daughter. He had also told her a lot of tales about her daughter, even saying that Yunma was "treacherous." He told her to be wary of her. Yunma intended to ignore Yuanpu's words, for she thought he must have been mentally ill—a condition caused by old age. Furthermore, he was just telling tales about her: this didn't hurt her. But Yuanpu became more and more peculiar—and more intensely so. Later, he not only went upstairs four or five times during the day, but he also rapped on her mother's door at midnight. This wasn't a problem for him, of course, because for decades he had slept very little at night, and yet he still had a lot of energy. But it troubled her mother a lot: once awakened, she couldn't go back to sleep. After several days of this, the old woman could no longer bear it, and so she had packed her things and returned to the countryside. Not long after that, she died. And so Yuanpu's relationship with Yunma immediately took a turn for the worse.

Irritated, Yunma turned deathly pale as she spoke. Sitting there, Jinglan kept sensing something spooky in this room. He shivered: Who in fact was lying? He squirmed uneasily in his chair.

"Six months ago, he began insisting that he had to have his bowel movements in his room. He said that he couldn't walk easily and couldn't use the toilet. But nothing was wrong with him: one night, I saw him go upstairs, just as fast as a thief! He did this in order to punish me. Tell me: How can I continue staying here?"

At this point, Yunma was staring at Jinglan, as if waiting for his answer. Jinglan thought it over and over and then said irresolutely, "I don't know. I can't help you. Sorry. I'm inexperienced in this kind of thing. Maybe you should talk it over with him. Or maybe I could ask a doctor to come. It seems he's become a little obtuse."

"Do you believe doctors?" Yunma's eyes shone. "Let me tell you: you must never believe doctors! It was a doctor's cure that killed my mother. If she hadn't left . . ." Suddenly terrified, she stopped talking.

When Jinglan walked out of Yunma's room, he saw a hand closing Yuanpu's door across the hall. Who could that be? Jinglan suddenly got it, and he turned back to say to Yunma: "Was he outside listening to us?"

"Naturally. There's no way to keep anything from him." Yunma smiled faintly.

As he walked along the road, Jinglan felt uneasy. The shadows of the house shrouded his mind. His respected mentor had actually reached this stage. He had never expected this. He felt obligated to help him, but unfortunately Yuanpu didn't want his help. Maybe he was even mocking him for not understanding the world! Hadn't Yunma also felt that he was ridiculous? Anyhow, he must give up the idea of helping Yuanpu. Then Jinglan began doubting his former impressions of Yuanpu. Over the decades, his mentor had never appeared decrepit in spirit. He loved arguing, never wearying of it. While arguing, his very being glowed with an unusual luster. Jinglan was always involuntarily drawn to his mentor's brilliance. And so, although Jinglan had left here years earlier, he still came back once a year. Actually, his mentor was the only person he couldn't leave behind. Could it be that his former impressions were all false? How could someone like Yuanpu have lost his mind? The configuration of Yuanpu's brain rose before Jinglan's eyes. He saw a tree whose leaves had all fallen. Its trunk and branches could be distinguished clearly, for they were bare. This kind of person was anything but out of his mind. But which image revealed the real Yuanpu? Was it the one who sat at his desk and thought all day and night? Or was it the one who dozed on the chamber pot and tiptoed like a thief through the house? He definitely couldn't believe what Yunma said; it was likely all slanderous. But her motive didn't seem to be to slander Yuanpu; it seemed more likely that she meant to scare Jinglan and make fun of him. What sort of confused state had Yuanpu's life turned into? Jinglan thought, too, that he shouldn't trust what he'd seen with his own eyes. His mentor was still as strong as an indestructible city wall. He could sense this while sitting in front of him, even though he had changed on the outside.

＝＝

Jinglan had already spent nine days in his hometown. Every day he went to the riverside and sat on the flood-control dike to look at the distant sails. Deep down, he felt a little at loose ends, and he also felt some melancholy that he couldn't dispel. These last few days he hadn't gone back to see his mentor, and he kept reproaching himself. The river here was a little old and its water was dark. But Jinglan could see its energy in the strength the boatmen exerted to row the boats. He knew this river well. First thing this morning, he'd been uneasy because he would leave this evening. At about noon, what he'd been expecting occurred at last. The man approaching him was Yunma's cousin.

"He's going to die in a couple of days." Both his facial expression and his tone were indifferent.

"What happened?" Jinglan asked.

On the way to the house, Jinglan was on the verge of tears, but in the end he didn't cry. Upon entering the house, Yunma's cousin went directly to the kitchen, where a lot of people were gathered. When Jinglan went into the bedroom, he saw Yuanpu sitting on the bed, repairing a lock. All kinds of small tools were spread out on the quilt. Jinglan let out a sigh.

"Did they ask you to come?" Yuanpu asked without raising his head. "Don't worry. I won't die. I just fell. It isn't serious. I fooled all of them. As soon as they came in, I pretended to be on my last legs."

"But when I came in, you didn't do that."

"That's because I knew it was you. When I saw Yunma's cousin go out, I guessed you would come."

He finally finished repairing the old-style copper lock and opened it a few times with the key. Then he put it and the tools into an iron box which he placed beside the bed. He looked toward the door and made a face, signaling Jinglan to open the door a crack.

The courtyard was noisy: a large coffin was being carried in. Yunma directed the porters to place the coffin under the oil-cloth rain shed. Jinglan noticed that she was dressed all in black. She looked refined and clean.

"This time, your joke has gone too far." Jinglan turned around and said, frowning in disgust.

"It doesn't matter. Yunma is an old hand at this. In the end, will it be she or I who wins this battle of wits? What do you think? This issue is just like a lock and this key. I think you'd better leave. This kind of environment is hard on you. And don't come back next year, either. Why make yourself uncomfortable? Come, help me shift my legs a little. I'm already dead from the waist down because of my fall, yet my upper body is still vigorous."

His legs were very heavy, bewilderingly so. Even when he shoved them energetically a few times, Jinglan couldn't move them. All he could do was climb into the bed, bend down, and shift them with both hands. His face turned purple. After he had arranged Yuanpu's legs and covered them with a quilt, he and Yuanpu looked at each other. He noticed that Yuanpu's eyes were a little damp, and he felt his emotions surge.

"Go on, go on! Why haven't you left yet?!" Yuanpu was energetically waving his hand, perhaps to cover his embarrassment or perhaps because he was weary.

Jinglan walked into the courtyard, where Yunma had just arranged the coffin. Looking at Jinglan, she gave him an unearthly smile. She said, "Come back again next year. Mr. Yuanpu always cares about you."

"This . . ."

"Do you mean the coffin? This is just for looks. How can he die? He can fool the others, but he can't fool me. Are you going now? Come back next year for sure. For sure! You're all he thinks of!"

Jinglan quickened his pace, but Yunma was behind him, seeing him off. She was excited. She opened her mouth a few times, wanting to say something, but in the end she said nothing. She just silently watched Jinglan walk into the distance.

=====

As Jinglan got back to the street, he thought he had no reason to despise Yunma. He had seen that his mentor seemed content with his lot in that eerie house; it was hard for others to understand what was so wonderful about his life. It seemed that Jinglan himself now had no choice but to consider himself one of the others. After all, he returned only once a year. Although he had thought of himself as his pupil, in the end, he hadn't mastered some things—for instance, he didn't understand Yuanpu's relationship with Yunma at all. He could only understand the Yuanpu of the past—and evidently there was no connection between the mentor of the past and the mentor of the present. Had this change occurred only when he had a premonition that he would die soon?

Jinglan kept going, intending to thrust all of this behind him. Then he changed his mind and decided to board the boat and leave at once. He walked to the wharf. As it happened, a boat was waiting. No sooner had he entered the cabin and fallen onto the cot than the boat started up. Half-dazed, he heard the water grumbling below and felt it was a little absurd to have left immediately.

At midnight, he awoke with a start and walked onto the deck. When he looked up, he saw a large meteor fall from the sky. He looked down: everything was inky black. The events of the past few days once more weighed heavily on his heart. The boat had already gone a long way. For some reason, Jinglan felt that this was not like leaving, but instead like sailing straight toward the dark center of his hometown. It was a place where he'd never been before.

The gigantic owl—twice as large as ordinary owls—had been coming around for days, each time at dusk. It sat on a branch of the old mulberry, its round eyes—of indeterminate color—like two demonic mirrors.

That day, Mrs. Yun returned from the vegetable garden carrying a pair of empty buckets on her shoulders. As she turned and suddenly saw this big thing, her legs went weak and she nearly fell. She wanted to run off, but she couldn't move. It was as if something were holding on to her legs. She struggled for a long while and calmed down only when she reached her door. When she looked again at the tree and saw that thing again, she promptly shut the courtyard gate.

Mr. Yun was sharpening a hatchet. She noticed a ruthless expression looming on his face.

"What scared you so much?"

Walking over, he opened the courtyard gate and watched for a while.

"Hunh!" he said.

Then he closed the gate slowly. Mrs. Yun knew he didn't feel like talking. And because of his explosive temper, she didn't dare ask him anything. She heard the chickens hopping around uneasily in the coop. One old hen didn't want to return to her nest. Finally, she grabbed the hen and thrust it in. With that, all twelve chickens in the coop went crazy, and Mrs. Yun's heart thumped continuously. She remained in shock right up until she lit the lamp, finished her dinner, and washed the dishes. She wanted to open the courtyard gate to take another look, but she didn't have the nerve.

Sure enough, that night the chickens and dogs were all in an uproar. The next morning, two chickens were missing. At the gate were chicken feathers and traces of blood. Mrs. Yun thought, *was it the owl?* Why did she think it was a man-eating beast? Mr. Yun looked at the feathers on the ground and said, "This doesn't matter."

Feeling uncertain, she stood next to the entrance, cupped her hands, and shouted through her tears: "Wumei! Wumei!"

She was calling her daughter. She'd had five children, but the first four had died. The only one left was Wumei. Her daughter leapt out from the dry ditch; she had cut a small bundle of firewood.

"What are you shouting about?" Wumei said disapprovingly. Her face was flushed.

Mrs. Yun reproached her: "What are *you* shouting about?"

Wumei set the firewood down and went to her room. Mrs. Yun knew she was making papercuts again. Recently, she'd become infatuated with a weird design—concentric circles. She cut them out of black paper and pasted them on the walls and windows. Mrs. Yun told her that looking at the rings made her dizzy. But Wumei didn't care and continued cutting.

Mrs. Yun was a little indignant because no one else in the family was upset by what had happened the night before. And neither father nor daughter seemed to think the ill-omened bird was even there. They just went on doing whatever they had to do. She wasn't one to make a mountain out of a molehill, but wasn't it true that something had invaded her life? Those two hens were both new and were about to lay eggs. They had eaten a lot of food every day.

Sulking, Mrs. Yun began making a commotion with the dishes in the kitchen.

"Just ignore it. Isn't it the same as if it weren't here?" Wumei said in a low voice.

She was standing next to the door, her eyes wide open. Mrs. Yun couldn't figure out what her bright black eyes were saying. She merely thought that her daughter was becoming more and more bewildering.

"What do you mean? It's obviously in that tree. And we've obviously lost two hens."

"We can raise more chickens."

With that, she walked away.

Mrs. Yun got goose pimples at the thought of Wumei's black rings. And so she sighed to herself: "Ah, she's destined to survive."

Mr. Yun went to the market with a load of hemp sandals. Mrs. Yun went to the farm to pull weeds. She didn't ask Wumei to go along.

As soon as she opened the door, she saw it. Now it was coming in the daytime, too. What a cruel thing! What should she do? She thought and thought, but could find no way to deal with the situation. *Whatever will be, will be,* she concluded. After closing the courtyard gate, she went to the farm.

It was an overcast day. Mrs. Yun kept listening uneasily. If there was any movement, she could run home at once. But nothing happened all morning. When she went home, it had left the tree. For some reason, Mrs. Yun felt that without the owl the tree was a little lonely and was standing there listlessly. Had she been affected by her daughter?

Nothing happened that night.

═══

Now Mrs. Yun was sitting in the doorway, stitching soles for cloth shoes, and the gigantic bird was in the tree across from her. The afternoon before, it had pecked a piglet to death—a tragic scene.

Mrs. Yun reminded her husband of her father's hunting rifle. Mr. Yun took the gun in his hands, looked around for a long time, and then put it down again. He said stiffly, "It's useless."

"Why? Why?" Mrs. Yun said impatiently, "Nothing's wrong with this rifle. Last year, Yun Bao killed a lot of wild rabbits with it. It's a good rifle."

"Is this a wild rabbit?" Mr. Yun roared fiercely.

"Then, what do you think it is? It's going to do us in." Mrs. Yun was furious.

"It is—it is—*bah!!*"

Mr. Yun went to the kitchen and started the fire.

Mrs. Yun's eyes blurred as she stitched the soles. It was as if the end of the world was coming. It took a long time for her to compose herself. She saw Wumei walk past the ditch with a basket on her arm. She was cutting pig fodder. She wasn't the least bit afraid, nor was she concerned about the family's losses. This child was a little callous. Whenever she told her anything, she said the same thing: "Just ignore it." But Mrs. Yun noticed that her daughter had changed: when she cut firewood and pig fodder, she no longer went far away, and she seemed to be detouring around that evil bird. Mrs. Yun was a little excited by this discovery. Father and daughter were not ignoring this issue, after all. Could they figure out what to do? As a housewife, she knew she couldn't make the decision in such a serious matter. She could only worry. When she looked again at the owl, it seemed bigger: it looked like a tiger sitting there.

From the kitchen came the sound of Mr. Yun singing mountain ballads. He seemed emotional. When he was young, he'd been good at singing these ballads. He was an educated person from the city, yet he had voluntarily settled down in the countryside. Mrs. Yun had come with him. Life in the countryside was quiet and dull, but because Mr. Yun liked it, Mrs. Yun subsequently came to like it, too.

Mr. Yun hadn't sung for a long time. Now, hearing him, Mrs. Yun couldn't sit still. She ran into the kitchen and started making pancakes.

"Are you making pancakes?" Mr. Yun was a little surprised.

"We have to celebrate!" Mrs. Yun said decisively.

"Oh, good point!"

The pancakes smelled delicious!

Wumei came home, and the three of them sat around the table eating pancakes. Mr. Yun was in a great mood; he even drank a glass of wine. Wumei had some wine, too, and her face glowed red. Looking at Mrs. Yun, she widened her eyes and said: "Are you going to leave us, Mama?"

"What?" Mrs. Yun thought she'd heard wrong. "What did you say?"

"Sorry, I shouldn't have said that." Wumei lowered her head and whimpered.

"She's had too much to drink," Mr. Yun said. "Why don't you have a little, too?"

And so Mrs. Yun also took a glass of wine.

Mrs. Yun seldom drank; when she left, she was a little dizzy. Carrying a bamboo basket, she went out to pick beans. She had just reached the turn when she was ambushed. She was aware of a lot of whips lashing her body. Since she couldn't avoid them, all she could do was roll around on the ground. She wondered if she would die. The bird was on top of her. How had it grown so many whips? Some struck her ruthlessly, as if hacking her body into two halves. She heard her tragic wail spread in the distance. After a while, she fainted; before she plummeted into darkness, she saw a terribly bright fireball.

When she sat up, she was in so much pain that it was like being pricked by needles. She moaned. From behind, someone pulled her up by her armpits. She screamed in pain, but she was steady on her feet. Ah, this was a middle-aged man, a stranger. When she looked at him again, though, she thought she'd seen him before. She remembered: when she was young, there was a handsome young man who had repaired cart tires at the roadside for a living. This one looked much like him, but was much stronger.

Mrs. Yun was a little excited.

"Are you Youlin?" she asked. Her voice quivered from pain.

"Yes. And you're Xiumei." As he spoke, his eyes roved. "That evil bird wants to destroy you."

"How did you happen to come here?"

"Why not? I often do. It isn't far."

"Not far from where?" Mrs. Yun looked at him in astonishment.

"My home. It's nearby."

"Your home?"

"Yes. Over there." He was pointing toward the wasteland behind him.

It finally occurred to Mrs. Yun that she'd been leaning against Youlin all along. Was he really that Youlin? Why didn't she feel at all shy? He supported her weight as she walked, and after she took a few mechanical steps, her pain subsided. Walking west, they crossed the wasteland and came to a vast swale. Mrs. Yun whispered to herself: *Did he actually live in the marsh?*

"Do you have a job, Youlin?"

"The same as before—fixing tires. That's all I can do."

"How can there be anyone in this wasteland who needs tires repaired?"

"There are always one or two. You haven't noticed them. When it's nearly sunset, they come over from the marsh."

"The marsh?! No one can walk in it."

"They're light. They can walk over from above."

At first, Mrs. Yun had been a little excited by leaning against a man she had dreamed of in her youth. Now, all of a sudden, it was as though she'd been splashed with cold water. She wanted to break loose from him, but when she tried, she was pressed even closer to him. Slowly, she began to desire him, but this feeling also frightened her. Her arms lengthened and tightly entwined him.

"Then, can you also walk over from above?" Her voice was trembling.

"Ah. Yes."

They could see the marsh and an apple tree there. Youlin's tools hung from a fork in the tree, and the chrome-plated wrench flashed with light. Looking at this scene, Mrs. Yun felt glum. But this didn't hold her longing within limits.

They sat down to rest under the apple tree. Birds were squabbling fearfully in the marsh. Mrs. Yun noticed a tiny grave with a tombstone on it. Mrs. Yun asked Youlin whose it was and how a tomb could be built in a marsh. Youlin was thinking back on something. After a while, he finally answered, "Him."

Mrs. Yun was no longer in pain, but she was growing feverish. She heard Youlin say, "Let's take off our clothes." It seemed to be someone else speaking. After hesitating a moment, she began undressing. So did Youlin. Holding each other, they walked toward the marsh. Strictly speaking, Youlin dragged Mrs. Yun over there.

The sun was shining, and the water was warm. Sex in the marsh wasn't like real sex. There was only extreme longing, but she felt no great pleasure. At first, Mrs. Yun thought she would sink, but the damp earth beneath her was buoyant. Their bodies were half-buried in it, but they didn't sink down. She embraced him tightly. She felt he was confident in his knowledge of the earth here.

When they went back to the apple tree, some leeches were sticking to their bodies. Mrs. Yun abhorred them, beat them hard, and got rid of two of them. She dressed. Five were sticking to Youlin, but he didn't care. Nor did he get dressed. He sat on a rock, casting his eyes at the marsh in the distance. Mrs. Yun thought he had forgotten her. Anyhow, what were they to each other? Mrs. Yun couldn't think it through at this moment. When she looked up, she saw a lot of black rings on the apple tree, one ring within another—much like Wumei's papercuts. She thought of asking this man what was hanging on the tree, but when she saw his expression, she abandoned the idea.

"I have to go home. I'm a little afraid of that bird."

"Then I'll walk you home."

Youlin got dressed and walked behind her in silence. Mrs. Yun walked rapidly. When she passed the mulberry opposite her front door, she didn't see the bird. There was just a pile of bird droppings on the ground. Mrs. Yun went through the courtyard gate, and when she turned around, Youlin had disappeared.

Mr. Yun and Wumei were playing Chinese chess in the courtyard. Mrs. Yun raised her voice and said: "Who among our villagers has ever gone to the marsh?"

Mr. Yun stretched, stood up, and said: "No one. But at night, outsiders have come out from there. I've heard that people and carts are coming and going all the time. But I've never seen what actually goes on there."

Mrs. Yun looked at her husband in disbelief and went into the kitchen without a word.

As she cooked, Mrs. Yun tried hard to remember how she had reached the marsh. It was at least twelve miles from the village. How had she been able to make the round trip in such a short time—as if she had flown? If it was always so easy, then wasn't it as if Youlin lived at her front door? She felt she'd made a mistake and thought there might be problems later. Back then, in her hometown, she hadn't fallen in love with Youlin. Where on earth had he come from now? Was this person really Youlin?

At night, when the moon shone into the bedroom, Mr. Yun had already been in and out of many dreams. All of a sudden, Mrs. Yun woke up and heard some movement in the next room. Without even bothering to put on her shoes, she rushed out.

"Wumei! Wumei!"

Shivering, she groped for a match on the windowsill and lit the lamp. The bed was empty. Where was Wumei? Ah, she was squatting next to the bureau. She stood up and covered half of her face with her hand.

"What happened to your face?"

"Leave me alone!"

Mrs. Yun suddenly pulled her hand away from her face. Then she retreated two steps in fright, for half of her daughter's face had disappeared, as if it had been cut off with a knife!

"Oh! Yunshan! Yunshan!!" Mrs. Yun screamed for her husband.

"You are so ignorant."

With that, Wumei calmly walked out.

In the lamplight, Mrs. Yun noticed black rings all over the room, some moving in the air, others attached to the walls. Several were even hanging from the beams. Mr. Yun came into the room; he seemingly didn't care about these black rings. He stood motionless in the middle of the room.

"Wumei . . . her face . . ." Mrs. Yun stuttered.

"Ha, this little thing! Her hoaxes are becoming more and more brilliant. Just ignore her."

"What attacked her . . . Was it that bird?"

"Maybe. But don't you worry about her. She's destined to survive."

"Destined to survive?"

Taking her doubts with her, Mrs. Yun went back to bed. In the dark, she asked Mr. Yun: "Do you remember Youlin, who repaired tires on the corner of Dragon Street?"

"Sure. I had him repair tires for me. He went north a long time ago when some of his relatives asked him to run a factory there."

"But I've seen a man much like him here. How can someone look so much like him? Even his voice is the same."

Mr. Yun seemed to be snickering. After a while, Mrs. Yun heard him snoring.

The gigantic bird was still sitting in the tree, but it had been several days since it had attacked any of the family's livestock. What was it doing sitting up there? Mrs. Yun thought it must be very hungry; green light flashed from its eyes even though it was daytime. Mrs. Yun sometimes thought of detouring around it, but she couldn't stop herself from walking over there again. Once, she was so frightened when she looked up that she almost plopped down on the ground. After a while, a thought came to her: "Is it possible that this thing wants to eat me?" When she turned around and took another look, it had closed its eyes. She regretted having approached it just then—it was too risky.

In the cool early morning breeze, Mrs. Yun stood next to the kidney bean vine and recalled meeting Mr. Yun years earlier for the first time. His family had moved from far away to the town where her family lived. It was a long time before people in the neighborhood became aware of their existence, because the family didn't talk much with others—and because they delivered coal for a living. City people generally did not make friends with coal deliverymen. When he was young, Mr. Yun was rather thin, not as robust as he was now. One time he was pulling a cart of coal up the steepest incline on the neighboring street. It was drizzling and his tires skidded. He kept climbing up and sliding down. Mrs. Yun was watching from one side. Probably it was the eighth or ninth time that he slipped down that Mrs. Yun couldn't bear to watch any longer. She rushed up and helped him push the cart. Then the two of them went up the slope together. Little did she think that Mr. Yun would stop the cart and angrily rebuke her for meddling. Mrs. Yun blushed, glared at him in disdain, and left.

Before long, Mr. Yun invited her to a movie. When he was young, Mr. Yun was very handsome. How could Mrs. Yun turn him down? Later, she discovered that Mr. Yun was generally amiable, but if one interfered with his work, he immediately turned harsh. He couldn't put up with any comments on his work. During those years on Dragon Street, Mrs. Yun saw her husband toiling and wanted him to hire a helper, but he sternly refused. He went to work on time every day and never asked for time off. Even when he was sick, he wouldn't let Mrs. Yun help. When he pulled the cart, his body became one with the cart. Even Mrs. Yun felt there was no room for another person in this scene. Mrs. Yun joked with him and nicknamed him "Charcoal." She felt all along that he pulled the cart not only to support the family but also for another reason. What on earth was this other reason?

She observed him working under the blazing sun. The black-top roads were boiling hot. Drop by drop, his sweat fell onto the ground. His eyes were wide open and his face a little pale. Mrs. Yun thought he would have heat stroke, but she also knew that he was engrossed in daydreams and so she shouldn't disturb him. From years of experience, Mrs. Yun knew that the more strain he was under, the more excited he was. And so the one time that she had helped him push the cart had amounted to depriving him of pleasure.

As Mrs. Yun saw it, after marriage, their life on Dragon Street was neither all gloomy nor was it all sweetness and light. The two of them lived a simple, austere life. Mrs. Yun loved children. Who could have imagined that she would fail to bring up her children? Even now, she need only close her eyes and she could see her four darling children. Because of them, Mr. Yun and she were both drained of tears. Mr. Yun advised her to abandon the idea of having more children, but she wasn't convinced. Mr. Yun said, "The air here is poisonous." Suddenly one day, he loaded up the cart with a lot of household goods and said that he wanted to live with relatives in the countryside. Although Mrs. Yun couldn't comprehend what life in the countryside would be like, she did want to be far away from this place where she was grieving. And so she ignorantly came along with Mr. Yun. Their move should have been considered a success, for didn't they later have Wumei? As a child, Wumei was really lovable, and Mrs. Yun felt delirious with love. But this child became more and more somber. It was hard for Mrs. Yun to communicate with her. At first, she was a little offended, but she gradually came to understand her a little. The little girl was a lot like her father; still, she worried about her. This heaven-sent treasure was the triumphant result of Mr. Yun's decision. This led her to recall the way Mr. Yun looked when he hauled the coal up the hill on that rainy day.

Because Wumei was grown up now, Mr. Yun no longer liked to talk much, and it was always quiet and cheerless at home. Sometimes when Mrs. Yun was cooking, she felt as though no one lived here. To reassure herself, she sometimes had to check out the courtyard. She always saw father and daughter silently doing their own things. Mrs. Yun knew they both still loved her; they just didn't express it well. They were too absorbed in their own concerns. Take this bird, for example. At first, Mrs. Yun thought it was an ordinary bird, but father and daughter didn't see it that way. They had much more profound insights. Mrs. Yun was only dimly aware of their worlds.

After picking the kidney beans, Mrs. Yun headed home, for she had to boil congee with kidney beans—something the whole family loved. The courtyard was empty; both father and daughter had gone to the field. When Mrs. Yun laid eyes on the chicken coop, she was horrified to see the bird standing there. Oddly, the chickens were walking back and forth, not at all afraid. Ah! Could it be that it had come to deal with her?

Mrs. Yun went back to the kitchen, thinking the future was boundless. As she lit the fire and chopped vegetables, her hands shook violently. She was on constant alert, afraid that the bird would pounce at any moment. Though she was under a lot of strain, she remembered the question that had been nagging her all along. Mr. Yun had sacrificed for her the work that he loved and had turned to plaiting hemp sandals. Deep down in his heart, could he resent this? But he didn't seem to. He seemed satisfied and self-sufficient. When Wumei showed him her papercuts, he would stare at the black rings and say, "Great! Great!" Mrs. Yun recalled that he had never resented anything. Was he the sort who believed in "taking things as they come"?

The congee boiled with fresh kidney beans was wonderful, and the three of them ate with gusto. Mrs. Yun noticed nothing different in either father or daughter.

"That ruffian has occupied the chicken coop. What should we do about the chickens?" she finally spoke.

"You worry too much," said Mr. Yun.

"Huh?"

Mrs. Yun angrily cleared away the bowls and chopsticks. She had no way to pour out the pain in her heart to anyone, so she came up with some malicious ideas. When she was working in the kitchen, she laughed grimly every few minutes. Meanwhile, she made time to look inside the chicken coop to see if the bird was still there. It was so bulky that it occupied half the henhouse. The green light shooting from its eyes was murderous. Why weren't the chickens afraid of it? Had they reached an agreement?

When Wumei entered the kitchen, Mrs. Yun asked her: "Did your father bring the bird in? Will we have to live with it from now on?"

"I think it came in by itself. I'm going to ignore it."

Actually, Mrs. Yun also thought that it had come in by itself, but she couldn't suppress the wrath she felt toward her husband. When she fed the pigs, they were also calm, as if they weren't at all affected by their proximity to the formidable enemy. Mrs. Yun thought, *Maybe there won't be a problem, after all?* Anyhow, the answer would be clear at dusk when the chickens went back to the coop. She forced herself to be a little more patient.

Father and daughter left. The courtyard was quiet. The hens were all sleeping soundly in the sunshine, now and then making nonsensical *gugu* sounds. Just one hen was taking a bath in the sand. It didn't seem to be at all on guard. Mrs. Yun swept the courtyard. Only after sweeping all the corners did she sweep the henhouse. Suddenly, locking gazes with the bird, she went numb all over. She couldn't move. She and the bird stared at each other for a long time. Finally, one of them turned away. After Mrs. Yun recovered her wits, she found her clothing drenched with perspiration.

At dusk, things took a turn for the better. The owl swaggered out of the henhouse and stood in the courtyard for a few seconds. The chickens and ducks all stopped what they were doing to watch the big bird. With a *hu* sound, it flew away, its huge wings raising dust and sand from the ground. Mrs. Yun hurried to the doorway at once and saw it stop on the tree again. Father and daughter were walking along the ditch near the tree. But it wasn't just the two of them. Someone else was there, too. Because he was wearing a straw hat, she couldn't immediately recognize him. Ah, it was Youlin! He parted from them at the tree and took the road to the market.

"You came back with our former neighbor," Mrs. Yun said.

"He's very smart. Right off the bat, he seized the chance to do business next to the marsh. He has it together a lot more than we do." Mr. Yun appraised the figure that was receding in the distance.

"What kind of work does he do?" Mrs. Yun blurted out. Actually, she wanted to stop herself, but couldn't.

"It's hard to say what goes on in the marsh. I've heard only rumors."

Father and daughter sat down calmly in the courtyard and played chess, as if there was nothing to worry about. After making tea for them, Mrs. Yun went back to the kitchen. Today's events had left her at a loss. It seemed that a distance of about twelve miles wasn't so far: this person could come over whenever he wanted. Maybe he lived next to the village. How could this tire repairman and the Dragon Street scene have become entangled with her? Ever since leaving that unjust place, Mrs. Yun had felt that her family had broken completely with it. Yet, not only was it not a complete break, but it was possible to have frequent contact. She had simply been unaware of this. It was such a sinister world.

"It's so scary to repair tires for people in the marsh," said Wumei. "What I'm most afraid of is pushing a cart on the marsh."

"Have you seen it?" Mrs. Yun asked lightly.

"Once when I was a child. But the people in the carts were prisoners on their way to being executed. I didn't dare look and began to cry."

"Nonsense. When did you go to the marsh? I don't remember that."

Mrs. Yun thought to herself, *How can this child run off at the mouth like this?* She'd been such a good child. Making up stories like this: Could it be that she found Youlin revolting?

"Those prisoners all had long beards, and the tops of their heads were like stumps that had been chopped off. The cart drivers were all very ugly. One was an old ape."

"Do you remember who took you to the marsh?"

"No. It must have been Daddy."

After Wumei left, several black rings were visible on the spot where she'd been standing; they were like cauterized imprints. Mrs. Yun scuffed them with her foot but couldn't get rid of them. When she took a closer look, she didn't see them.

They were eating supper. After Mrs. Yun changed the lamp wick, the kerosene lamp brightened. Mrs. Yun noticed that the father's and daughter's faces flickered in the lamplight, and a dark shadow stood behind Mr. Yun for a while and then behind Wumei for a while. Mrs. Yun forgot about eating. All of a sudden, she burst out: "Youlin?" She was scared out of her wits.

"Living where Youlin lives isn't as tough as we imagine. I suppose there are some arcane truths there. Let's drop this subject. I'm afraid it will frighten Wumei," Mr. Yun said.

Wumei's shining eyes led Mrs. Yun to think of the strange bird's eyes.

"Give me some credit, will you, Daddy?"

"Could Youlin be dead?" Mrs. Yun said.

Mr. Yun began laughing. Mrs. Yun saw the dark shadow behind him bow in his direction.

"No way. You just saw that he was all right, didn't you? I told you: he has a great life! I've thought about him in the years that we've been apart. But it never occurred to me that he was living next to the marsh. I used to haul coal, and he fixed tires. Back then, I felt that he and I were much the same. As I see it now, we are indeed in different social classes. Think about it: So many years have gone by, how could our characters not have changed?"

Mrs. Yun was staring at her husband's face, which had gradually become thinner. Her disbelief was growing. Mr. Yun seldom talked so much. What was wrong with him today? The dark shadow behind him seemed to be smelling his hair. Mrs. Yun wanted to stand up, but she felt nailed to her chair. Wave after wave of chills assailed her. She set her chopsticks down.

"Ma!" Wumei shouted.

"Ah?" She was a little more clear-headed.

"You have to give me some money to buy glossy paper."

"Oh, okay! You're so industrious."

Wumei stood up and went back to her room. Just then, the owl began hooting. It wasn't like the frightening hoot of an ordinary owl. It didn't scare Mrs. Yun at all; it was merely a little strange. It was intense and resounding, and it lasted a fantastically long time. She thought, *Maybe this is the birds' mountain ballad?* It was a long time before it stopped hooting.

Mrs. Yun lit another lamp and went to the courtyard gate to investigate. As usual, she was worried about her chickens and ducks, but there was no problem: it was quiet all around. Outside, the old mulberry tree bobbed its head gently in the breeze, and the owl was no longer there. Perhaps, its song had been its last outburst. What emotions did its outburst hold? Birds' ideas were hard to fathom. Two villagers passed by the tree. They were quarreling, and suddenly they came to blows. One of them lifted the older one into the ditch. Mrs. Yun heard the one in the ditch groaning loudly. Mrs. Yun called Mr. Yun over to help the old codger.

"It seems he doesn't want our help. Take a look for yourself. You'll see."

Mrs. Yun limped the whole way over there. A lot of stones and clods of earth were piled up on the path.

"Uncle Weng, do you want me to help you? Or do you want me to call someone over to help?"

She was talking to the blurry ball below, but it didn't answer. Quite the opposite: she heard a strange sound come from his mouth—like the menacing sound made by a cat when it encounters a suspiciously dangerous adversary. Frightened, Mrs. Yun turned and went home.

"What's wrong with Uncle Weng?"

She saw Mr. Yun snickering.

"I guess he's enjoying life in the ditch," Mr. Yun said.

"If I open the courtyard gate, will our chickens, ducks, and piglets be safe?"

"Hard to say. Nobody can be sure."

Mr. Yun went back to his room to plait sandals. He liked working at night. He would work until midnight.

Mrs. Yun took another look at the ditch. She heard nothing now. For some reason, she visualized a motorcade on the marsh. She muttered, "Something is coming closer and closer." When she went inside, her legs felt like lead.

Wumei told her that the last time she went to the market to sell papercuts, a group of women had surrounded her. They wanted a hundred of her works. Those countrified women seemed to come from a remote mountain area. There were two blind people among them.

"Did they buy your interlinked rings?" asked Mrs. Yun.

"Yes. They wanted to take them home and learn how to make the rings. When I asked where they came from, they just mentioned a strange place name. It definitely isn't in our province, and yet I could understand their accent. One of the older ones told me that the sun shines there all year long, so they like black and they like circles."

Mrs. Yun took stock of Wumei's bedroom wall. Now there were no longer black rings pasted there, but many yellow ants. Looking at them was nauseating. Wumei was truly spirited and skillful. Such tiny ants: she could cut them out so they were lifelike. But why didn't she cut some pleasant things?

Mrs. Yun was dazed as she stood in Wumei's room. Wumei was staring at her, obviously urging her to leave soon. Mrs. Yun couldn't imagine when Wumei had begun being so uncompromising. No matter what she was doing, she always had her own way. She sighed and went back to her own room.

The bedroom she shared with Mr. Yun was spacious. The old-fashioned bed with flowers carved on it was large, like a small house. When they first moved here, Mrs. Yun didn't feel comfortable. And so, every day after dinner, Mr. Yun extinguished the lamp, making the house as dark as a cave. Mrs. Yun gradually felt better in the dark. Back then, night birds—usually more than ten of them—always flew over to their windowsill. They were small, and their songs were soft and gentle like crickets on the stove. Mr. Yun joked that he had summoned the birds to keep Mrs. Yun company. Sure enough, these soft sounds at night soothed her nerves. Later, they stopped coming, and Mrs. Yun raised more chickens, because chickens could also dispel her inner unease. Especially the hens that laid eggs.

As she stitched the soles for cloth shoes, Mrs. Yun was thinking of the lovely events of the past. The strange thing was that when she thought of the bizarre episode between Youlin and her, she didn't feel guilty. She was merely curious. Occasionally, she thought that even if she told Mr. Yun about it, he probably wouldn't care. She felt that in the last two years, father and daughter were bewitched by something that she had no way to understand. Nothing else would have made such an impact on them.

All of a sudden, she felt sleepy. Mr. Yun was still plaiting sandals, so she went to bed first. She lay in bed for a while, but no longer felt sleepy. When she heard the window rattling, she got up to close it.

"Who's there?"

"Me. Youlin. I'm back from the market. I've brought some glossy paper for you."

After tossing a package through the window, he hurried off.

Mrs. Yun picked it up and looked at it carefully in the moonlight. This glossy paper should be purple; in the moonlight it looked a little wicked. She lit the lamp uneasily. Sure enough, it was purple. It was the best kind of glossy paper.

When Mrs. Yun went to Wumei's room, she was still awake. She was cutting those ants in front of the lamp. Mrs. Yun gave her the glossy paper. She said she'd bought it a few days before, but had chucked it into the kitchen cupboard and forgotten about it. She didn't know if the color was right.

"It's perfect. Did Uncle Youlin give it to you?"

"How did you know?"

"He said he wanted me to try the purple color."

Wumei took out a sheet of paper and began cutting right away. Mrs. Yun looked on tensely.

She cut out a centipede, and on the centipede's tiny foot she pasted even smaller centipedes. Twirling the scissors quickly, she explained her work: "These are eyes."

Feeling increasingly uncomfortable, Mrs. Yun left. She went back to bed and fell asleep after a while.

━━━

The day that Mr. Yun carried hemp sandals to the market, the weird bird didn't come over. But Youlin did. He spoke with Mrs. Yun at the courtyard wall.

"My business has been a little slow lately, but it still isn't bad," he said.

"What exactly is going on with the carts on the marsh? One has to see that kind of thing to believe it," Mrs. Yun said.

"That's too hard for you. It's too dangerous for a woman to be there in the middle of the night. Even a man like me is sometimes afraid."

"But you still stay there?"

"What I want to see hasn't happened yet."

"When you lived on Dragon Street, were you aware of our Plum Village? Back then, had you been to this marsh?"

"Dragon Street? No. The place where I used to live was 'Yuegu Street.' It was in the suburbs."

"What do you mean? Aren't you Youlin?"

"You can say that I am." He was a little down in the mouth as he looked at her.

"You yourself said you used to repair tires."

"I did repair tires."

"Why are you so laid back?!" Mrs. Yun howled furiously.

"I am a little laid back."

Mrs. Yun watched him lower his head and leave. She couldn't help feeling afraid. She looked up at the sky; it was yellow. Giving it some more thought, she realized that the frightening thing had occurred about fifteen miles away; her home should be safe. But she still felt perplexed and alarmed. The handsome repairman who formerly lived on Dragon Street—the object of girls' longing—no longer existed. The one she had run into was another person entirely. And she had become ludicrously involved with this other person. Probably the owl had flown over here from the marsh. But why was no one else afraid of it? Why was she the only one? Sometimes, she wanted to blot out the incident in the marsh, but that wouldn't do. Her family members and the phenomena all around pointed that way, as if they all wanted that incident to be pinned in her heart forever.

Wumei had pasted a centipede on the courtyard gate: Youlin must have seen it. The purple centipede had been chopped into two parts in the middle; there was only a threadlike connection between them. Had Wumei pasted it there for him to see? Could he possibly be seducing Wumei?

"Wumei, you work too late," Mrs. Yun said.

"I know, but I want to save money. People want my goods now, so I'd better make more of them. I'm afraid there won't be an opportunity later on."

"What are you saving money for?"

"To go far away. Isn't that what you and Daddy did?"

Dazed, Mrs. Yun looked at the blocked wall. She felt as if her heart had been hollowed out.

"Do you want to go to the marsh?"

"No. I've been there once. I want to go to a place where I've never been."

The beautiful Wumei held her head high, like a swan swimming past the wall.

Now only Mrs. Yun was left at home. The village was also quiet. There was only one old codger smoking as he sat under a tree. He was the Uncle Weng who had been dropped into the ditch. Uncle Weng was gesturing in the air with his pipe, as if arguing with someone. Five hens were bathing in the mud and dust at the wall; they looked very happy. Mrs. Yun made quick work of feeding the pigs, sweeping the courtyard, and mopping the floors in the house. Neither Wumei nor Mr. Yun would be home for lunch, and she had nothing more that she had to do. She stood distracted for a while in the courtyard. Then she couldn't keep from taking another look at the mulberry tree: the owl still hadn't returned. Uncle Weng was still sitting a little farther away. Mrs. Yun thought, *Maybe he's also waiting for the evil bird.*

Mrs. Yun went back to her room and sat down to stitch soles for cloth shoes. But she still felt uneasy. She felt that the peaceful phenomenon was nothing but an illusion. Recently, everything had changed irreversibly. Her Wumei was scheming to go far away. Of course this was a blow, but in her heart she also harbored a hope: maybe because of this her daughter would have a good future and be able to live the life she wanted. She thought, *Probably she met someone from a certain place through her papercuts, and so she began preparing to go away.* After all, she wasn't an uncontaminated village child. Her ideas were very complex. As she thought of this, she felt proud of her daughter, even though their relationship had recently been a little strained. She looked at the papercut centipede on the window. This was a particularly large one. She didn't know where Wumei had found such a large piece of glossy paper. The largest one at the market was one foot square, but this one was one foot two inches and deep purple. At first sight, this lifelike centipede was a little frightening. The most unsettling things were the little centipedes on the centipede's foot. For Wumei to have cut such a design, she must be harboring devilish ideas.

"Mrs. Yun! Mrs. Yun!"

Uncle Weng was calling her! Mrs. Yun rushed out of the house. At a glance, she saw that a large part of the courtyard wall had collapsed. She called to Uncle Weng and asked where he was, and then ran over to the gap in the wall to look out. But Uncle Weng was nowhere to be seen. Where had he been when he called out to her? Taking another look at the demolished earthen wall, she saw two tracks in the mud and dust. A cart had rushed past, rammed this large gap in her courtyard wall, and then had disappeared without a trace. This person must despise her family in order to have done such a thing. Who hated her family? It seemed no one did. Mrs. Yun tidied up the mess with a spade and dustpan. Suddenly, she thought of something: it was Uncle Weng who had called out to her. He must know who had been pushing the cart! She put the spade down and set out for Uncle Weng's house.

Weng's wife was drying peppers in the courtyard. When she saw Mrs. Yun, she didn't hail her, but just stared at her.

"Is Uncle Weng home? We've had an accident at our house. The courtyard wall has been pushed over. I heard Uncle Weng calling me and ran out to look, but I didn't see him."

"He isn't home. Tell me frankly: Are you guilty of having done something very bad?" Her gaze was murderous.

"Me? No. Does this have something to do with what I did? Maybe the person accidentally rammed into my wall and then ran off," Mrs. Yun said in bewilderment.

"Hunh. Let's hope so."

Distracted, Mrs. Yun went back to the courtyard and continued shoveling the mud and dust with her spade. Suddenly, her gaze halted at something in the pile of dust. A large-bodied fledgling that didn't yet have feathers was struggling clumsily. Ah, a baby owl! It was inconceivable that the owl lived inside the earthen wall. Mrs. Yun bent down and shifted it to a heap of dried leaves at one side. The little thing sorrowfully swung its bald head back and forth and made a hoarse *sisi* sound. Leaning on the iron shovel, Mrs. Yun watched it and quickly associated this with something else. If this little thing had emerged from her courtyard wall, then had the large scary one emerged from here, too? More and more of these dark connected ideas crossed her mind, and she felt she was going crazy. No, she couldn't cruelly kill this fledgling, but she didn't want to raise it, either. Then, just let it live and die on its own. Probably its mother would come and feed it. Flustered and unable to go on spading the mud and dust, Mrs. Yun went home.

She sieved and cooked the rice. She thought and thought and still was uneasy, so she went back to the courtyard to check on the baby owl.

Oh, the fledgling had vanished without a trace. The gigantic bird squatted motionless on the old mulberry tree. Was the fledgling its child? Had it hidden it somewhere? Or was the fledgling unrelated? Mrs. Yun couldn't keep from walking over to it again. The woman and the bird gazed at each other. Mrs. Yun started feeling feverish: she and the owl had begun communicating in a bizarre way. The gigantic bird's faint green eyes brought a certain reality and calmness to Mrs. Yun's empty, desolate heart. Mrs. Yun was no longer afraid of it. She even rushed to say to it: *Wa, wa!* The bird still didn't move. Mrs. Yun thought it had discerned her deepest, innermost ideas. Actually, she herself didn't know exactly what those ideas were.

When she went back to the courtyard, she sighed, "Today is really a long day."

Wumei and Mr. Yun came back together. Mrs. Yun mentioned what had happened to the courtyard wall. Mr. Yun listened attentively as he ate. At last, he said lightly, "I noticed a long time ago that something was wrong with that wall. It warbles all the time."

"The wall can make sounds? Why haven't I heard it?" Mrs. Yun was puzzled.

"Because you haven't tried. When I make sandals at night, the sound is awful."

In high spirits, Wumei talked of her new discoveries. She said those women had returned, this time bringing four blind people along. The blind people were all experts at paper-cutting.

"Those designs . . . my God! No, I can't explain it. What are the designs?! As soon as I saw them, I couldn't say a word. For example, there are some feathers, but they aren't feathers. No, they definitely aren't feathers! They must be—"

Her eyes turned vacant. She was silent. When Wumei was like this, Mrs. Yun worried, but as usual Mr. Yun paid no attention. He always approved of Wumei.

Wumei washed the bowls. Mrs. Yun noticed that she was working like a puppet. She dipped her hands into the water for a long time without washing even one bowl.

The bird began calling. When she heard it, Mrs. Yun wept. She couldn't bear it. In her mind, she kept visualizing the fledgling which had stared at her with blind eyes and whose beak had opened so wide. Mrs. Yun covered her face with her apron; she could still see it clearly.

"Mama! Mama!" Wumei shouted, horrified.

Mrs. Yun squatted down. Wumei closed the windows and doors tightly; only then did the bird's whining weaken.

"Mama—oh, I love you!"

"I love you, too, sweetheart." Mrs. Yun stood up with difficulty. She was dripping with cold sweat.

"Mama, I was the one who caused the wall to collapse. I wanted to see what was inside it. I shouldn't have—I was too impulsive!"

"Where were you when the wall collapsed?"

"I ran off and later went to the market."

"I want to find that little bird."

"Its mother ate it."

"Ah, so you saw it all."

"I was hiding in the ditch. It was really shocking: the mother bird swallowed her baby bit by bit. Half-way through, she choked. I thought the mother bird would choke to death."

As Mr. Yun's footsteps sounded outside, mother and daughter both regained their composure. Wumei looked at her father, and acting as if nothing had happened, she went back to her bedroom.

"This might start happening frequently," Mr. Yun said.

"What?"

"I'm speaking of Wumei. She's getting gutsier."

Mrs. Yun didn't respond. She wanted to change her clothes because she was unbearably cold. When she left the kitchen, the bird's whining had stopped. As she changed clothes in the bedroom, she saw someone standing outside the window. It was Youlin. Saying "damn guy," she shut the window with a bang.

Mrs. Yun awakened in the middle of the night from a deep sleep. She heard the wind repeatedly slamming against the window, its howling incessant. She sat up and so did Mr. Yun.

Side by side, the two of them stood at the window and looked out.

In the moonlight, the willow trees planted in the courtyard the year before were being blown from side to side, all of them taking on an unearthly lavender color. Fluttering in the air were some weeds from who-knows-where. All of them were burning. "Will there be a fire? Will there be a fire?" Mrs. Yun asked in a quivering voice. She kept shaking her husband's arm. Mr. Yun was also looking on in disbelief.

"Where did the fire start? Why didn't we see any smoke?" he mumbled.

But he evidently didn't really want to know where the fire started, for he staggered back to bed.

After giving it some thought, Mrs. Yun put on a jacket and

went outside. When she opened the door, a gust of wind almost knocked her down. Burning weeds no longer floated in the air. Instead, the air from the wind held a transparent purity. The full moon was a little dazzling. Because it had never been so bright, its rays were tinged with purple. When Mrs. Yun was about to go back inside, she suddenly saw a woman with disheveled hair standing at the gap of the courtyard wall.

"Who are you??" Mrs. Yun shouted sternly. She was trembling all over.

"Wumei!" the woman wailed.

In her bedroom, Wumei—by fits and starts—told Mrs. Yun of the night's events. She and the women she'd seen at the market had arranged to meet tonight to take a bus to a valley in the north where expert paper cutters gathered. They said there was a lot of good, tough glossy paper there, made from a plant that grows on the mountain. Because the plant was inexpensive, the paper was also cheap, and so all the villagers made papercuts. Outsiders exclaimed over their extraordinary designs. At the market, when they showed her one design, Wumei had been speechless with astonishment. She and the women headed toward the marsh. After walking a long time, they had intended to board a bus they'd seen stopped along the road. All of a sudden, a woman ran up from the marsh shouting something. Running up to them, she pointed at Wumei and said repeatedly that she was a "traitor." At that point, the women began driving her away. They lifted her up, threw her to the ground, and kicked her head. They trampled her until she fainted. Then they went off on the bus.

"I'm fed up. Just leave me alone." She waved at Mrs. Yun.

═══

Mrs. Yun felt that her home was gloomy these days. Whenever Wumei had spare time, she shut herself up in her room and made papercuts. Mrs. Yun didn't know exactly what she was cutting, because she no longer hung up her papercuts. As soon as she finished one, she hid it.

"Wumei, it's been a long time since you've gone to the market to sell things," Mrs. Yun said gingerly.

"I haven't finished anything yet."

Although Wumei appeared serene, Mrs. Yun knew this was a pose.

Mr. Yun said, "It's good for a kid to experience some setbacks."

When he spoke, Wumei's face was expressionless.

Mr. Yun had already repaired the earthen wall; it looked as if it had never been damaged. The new wall wasn't like a new one, either: fine grasses were still growing on it, so that it was exactly like the old wall. Mr. Yun did this work at night. In the morning, Mrs. Yun stood dazed next to the courtyard wall. She heard only magpies singing in the trees.

As Mrs. Yun stood there stunned, Mr. Yun came up and said:

"The water in the marsh has been low for quite some time. Now the sun has dried it up so it's hard as rock. It's said that a road will be built on it."

"How can that be?"

"These years, anything is possible."

Mr. Yun said he had left a hole under the wall for birds to stay in. He pointed it out to Mrs. Yun. The hole was cleverly designed: its entrance was behind a rock, so if you didn't look carefully you wouldn't find it. Mrs. Yun thought to herself, *No wonder birds have been inside the wall.* Mrs. Yun hadn't noticed before that Mr. Yun had this skill. Maybe Wumei had inherited her skill from her father. When Mrs. Yun put her hand in the hole, she found it was so deep that you couldn't touch the bottom.

"Back in the beginning, I never imagined that I had married someone who was such a skilled craftsman," she said as she stood up.

The news of the marshland caused her to worry anew about Youlin, but after the road was built over there, his business would be better, wouldn't it? Was he willing do business next to the highway? If he liked roads, then why had he run off and set up shop in the marshland? Mrs. Yun thought it over every which way and still didn't understand.

"Mrs. Yun, the magpies are singing so cheerfully that there must be a happy event in your family!" Old Mrs. Weng said as she entered the courtyard.

The old woman smiled hypocritically, and she looked ugly and ferocious. Mrs. Yun was a little afraid of her.

"Old Weng is sitting in the ditch, waiting for that event!"

"What event?!" Mrs. Yun was startled.

"Something connected with the marsh. Lend me a little salt."

When Mrs. Yun went into the kitchen to get the salt, the old woman tagged along.

"Your Wumei is blissful," she said as she took the salt.

Mrs. Yun figured borrowing salt was her excuse to come and reconnoiter. She reeked of the strong smell of pepper and spices. It made one's thoughts run wild. After she left, Mr. Yun mockingly commented that she was "the flower queen." Mrs. Yun asked him why he called the old woman the "flower queen." Mr. Yun said, "Go ask Uncle Weng. He knows. Don't think of them just as neighbors. Their home is the barometer for this region."

"Why did she say that Wumei is blissful?" Mrs. Yun was very suspicious.

"Maybe she smelled out this omen with her nose."

Later, Mrs. Yun went to the pigpen to feed the pigs. As she listened to the pigs chewing their food, she heard the Wengs talking outside her pigpen.

"Lately, the situation kept changing. Now, it's finally come to light," Uncle Weng said.

"Then why don't you go check on it? The brushwood with the

floating wildfire is just where you're longing to be. As for me, I've smelled everything already."

"It's better to stay here without moving and let the roaring vehicles push across from the top."

"Yes, that makes sense."

Mrs. Yun wanted to continue listening, but they had already walked on. Only a few words carried by the wind reached her ears: "the low water season . . ."; "motorcade . . ."; "smoke . . ."; "prisoners . . ."; "before sunset . . ."; and so forth. Mrs. Yun set down her bucket and went out to look. She saw that they had already gone into their own courtyard. In this sort of dreary weather, Mrs. Yun didn't think Wumei would have any good luck; she was deeply uneasy about her daughter. The day before, Wumei had complained to her father that her brain was addled. "I can't cut anything new." Mr. Yun had advised her, "Leave your handicraft work and go walking in the mountains—the farther, the better. Don't be afraid of getting lost." When Mrs. Yun heard him say this, she wanted to slap him! She had no idea whether Wumei would do as her father suggested. In her mind, she kept seeing the piglet being cruelly killed.

The large pig stopped eating, swaggered to one side, and lay down. When Mrs. Yun looked closely, she saw a melancholy, sad expression in its eyes. She thought to herself: *Perhaps I should ask the vet to look at it.*

When she went to a neighboring village to look for the vet, he wasn't home. His wife said he had gone to the marshland first thing in the morning, because a large number of horses there had the pox and were lying on the ground braying and braying.

"One of our pigs is sick, too. There's also a sick pig at the Youshun household. They all caught it from over there."

As the vet's wife talked, she stared at Mrs. Yun, making Mrs. Yun so uncomfortable that she left immediately. She had walked some distance and yet she could still hear the woman shouting at her: "You need to calm down!" Mrs. Yun was really annoyed. She didn't want to go home, either, so she sat in a daze on a rock beside the field. When she had composed herself, she glanced all around. Everything was ashy and white. There was no vitality anywhere. Could the pox already be here? Growing worried again, she hurried home at once.

"There's a pestilence," she said.

Mr. Yun said "Oh" indifferently and continued sieving the rice. Noticing his livid face, Mrs. Yun knew something was wrong and headed for Wumei's room. Sure enough, Wumei was gone. Hanging from her mosquito net were little serpents that she had cut out.

"Has she really gone off?" a very upset Mrs. Yun asked her husband.

"Just ignore what she does. She's a child with ideas of her own. And the pestilence is everywhere, so how can she go on with her papercuts? It's better to hide for a while. One doesn't worry about what one doesn't see. A person alone won't be in danger. Last time, she shouldn't have gone with those other women."

Mrs. Yun glanced out the window with hopeless eyes and saw some villagers—old and young, men and women, some of them driving their pigs—hurrying past as though they were fleeing from disaster. Mrs. Yun recalled what she had heard the Wengs saying as she fed the pigs, and she thought even more that there was no way out. But what on earth was Mr. Yun up to?

"There's something wrong with the big pig," she said faintly.

"Oh, I saw that. I think it will survive."

Mrs. Yun felt that, in these days of pestilence, Mr. Yun's body had become heavy and unwieldy. Not only was he not as restless as others, but he had gradually become as solid as a rock. When he reached out for something, he was like someone exerting a lot of strength to open a massive iron door. The hens seemed to have sensed something, for they were especially afraid of Mr.

Yun. Whenever he went near them, they cried out in fear and flew high up in the air. Their wings stirred up dust and fluff and also lent energy to this lifeless courtyard. Only when Mr. Yun went to the pigpen to clean out the dung did the hens quiet down and shiver next to the wall. Mrs. Yun thought to herself, *Could he still do things that took strength, such as cleaning out the dung?* But she didn't want to go over to check. She was startled each time she heard her husband making loud noises.

Mrs. Yun steeled herself to go outside. She walked to the road, where she took hold of a child and asked where he was going. The child struggled hard, but she wouldn't let go of him.

"Tell me, and then I'll let you go!"

"I'm going to the marsh. I'm going to kill myself! So there!"

"Ah, don't go!"

"I have to! Let go of me . . ."

He bent down and began licking the back of her hand. His tongue was as quick as a serpent's. Nauseated, Mrs. Yun loosened her grip at once. The boy slid away like a billiard ball and ran off into the distance. After a while, he disappeared.

A motorcade appeared at the end of the road—foot-pedaled flat-bed trucks, with two or three people in each one. Not until the motorcade reached her did Mrs. Yun see that all of those people were tied up, and their faces were ashen. The drivers were all alike—rough, robust, heavily bearded guys from the countryside. Mrs. Yun immediately remembered what Wumei had told her. So this motorcade had come from the marshland. Mrs. Yun drew closer to get a better look at them; she wanted to see the prisoners' faces. She noticed that these prisoners were also very much alike; even their expressionless gazes were similar. You could say this expression was composed, or you could say it was indifferent. Suddenly she saw a familiar face. It was the vet. His expression was different from that of the prisoners: extreme yearning showed through his composure. He was also tied up, but he seemed to like this punishment: his face was as red as if he'd been drinking. As Mrs. Yun ran several paces after his truck, a jeer suddenly flashed out from his eyes. Mrs. Yun stood still. She craned her neck to see if Youlin was in the motorcade. He wasn't. He wasn't there.

She recalled, too, how the vet's wife had looked while she stared at her. Apparently, the villagers had all anticipated the present situation. She was the only one who was confused. Had Wumei really gone out on the mountain roads? Although the mountains around here were only some small hills and had no wild animals, this was still enough to make people uneasy. Mr. Yun said she had to "try a new path."

She saw that child. Head down, he was walking ahead, holding at his chest a large bird that had just grown feathers. Mrs. Yun thought it was the bird from the courtyard wall at her home.

"Hey, kid, why did you come back?"

"I forgot to take this bird with me."

With that, he scampered off.

Mrs. Yun glanced at the trees next to the road. Why had all the leaves turned an off-white color? Suspecting something was wrong with her eyes, she massaged them a few times and looked again: the leaves were still off-white. And not just the leaves, either: even the brown dog that she knew so well had turned into a gray dog. Her body felt as light as a swallow's wandering in an expanse of off-white scenery. The gigantic owl that she hadn't seen for a long time also appeared. It was watching her from the mulberry tree. Its eyes had turned into two points of cloudy white light. Its faded feathers looked old. When Mrs. Yun saw a rough bamboo pole lying on the ground, she was seized by a whim. She bent down and picked up the pole to drive away the owl. Although she tried several times, it didn't move. Just as she set the pole down and sat down to rest, she suddenly heard it cry out sadly. By the time she looked up, it had changed into a tiny black dot and vanished into a spot deep in the ashy white sky. Mrs. Yun was shaking from the depths of her being. Why was it so grief-stricken? Was it because it had lost its child? In the past, it had been so ferocious! An image of the docile piglet that had been killed came to Mrs. Yun's mind.

After cleaning out the pig dung, Mr. Yun sat in the courtyard shelling soybeans.

"Something's wrong with my eyes. Everything I see looks ashen," Mrs. Yun said.

"The same thing happened to me once, but it went away after a few days."

"Why didn't you ever tell me?"

"I was afraid you'd worry."

"The owl won't come back, will it?"

"No. Next time, it will be its son."

"I'm still worried about Wumei."

"No need to worry about her. Just take it as the old owl did. How much worse can it be?" This made sense to Mrs. Yun.

"Do you suppose the vet will return to the village?"

"Of course. But our pig is better now."

Mrs. Yun went to look at the pig right away. Mr. Yun had left food for it, and it was eating slowly at the trough. From a distance came the sound of trucks. Mrs. Yun didn't bother to go out to take a look. She quietly picked up a broom and swept the pigpen until it was perfectly clean.

After Mrs. Yun left the pigpen, she stood on a slope and looked into the distance. The colors of the things before her were gradually restored, and the sky was no longer so cloudy, either. As she stared into the distance, a shadow appeared in her field of vision. As she looked more closely and the shadow neared her, it grew more and more focused—and it even waved to her! Ah, it was Wumei! Where had she gone? The road she walked on seemed close and yet at the same time it seemed far away. Mrs. Yun could see even her backpack very clearly. Something seemed to be wrong with her legs: she was limping.

"W— u— u— m— ei—," she shouted.

Something blocked her voice. No matter how hard she tried, her voice wouldn't carry. Suddenly, she knew: Wumei was separated from her by several mountains. How could she see so well? It certainly was Wumei, because—for many miles all around—she had never seen anyone else with such a distinctive backpack. And there was also the way she walked—a little like a squirrel now. Mrs. Yun felt a twinge in her heart, and she almost lost her breath. She bent her head, and carrying the bucket, she went home.

"I saw Wumei," she said to Mr. Yun.

"So did I. After this, we'll see her often," Mr. Yun said insipidly.

"Is this all we get for bringing up a daughter?"

Mr. Yun laughed. "Isn't it true that your colored vision has also been restored?" he asked.

"You've been there, right?" She blinked her eyes and understood.

In Wumei's room, her mosquito net swayed in the breeze. Those small green serpents all seemed alive. They were moving around. Mrs. Yun looked at them woodenly, and her legs went weak for a while. Mr. Yun came over and led her out of the room, and then locked the door with a copper lock.

"We can see her whenever we want to," he said.

Mrs. Yun couldn't figure out her feelings: she seemed to want to weep and yet she seemed to rejoice.

Translators' Acknowledgments

We thank Bradford Morrow, editor of *Conjunctions*, for publishing three of the stories included in this volume: "An Affectionate Companion's Jottings" (No. 47, fall 2006); "Moonlight Dance" (No. 50, spring 2008); and "Rainscape" (No. 53, fall 2009). We also thank Heide Hatry for including "The Roses at the Hospital" in her book *Heads and Tales* (New York: Charta Art Books, 2009).

All of the other pieces appear here for the first time in English. We are grateful to Can Xue for graciously making available two stories that have not yet been published in Chinese, "Vertical Motion" and "Papercuts." We have worked with Can Xue for nearly ten years, and our association with her is one that we treasure.

We also wish to thank Open Letter's Chad W. Post and E.J. Van Lanen for their enthusiastic response to our submission of this book. We greatly appreciate E.J. Van Lanen's skill in editing this manuscript. He made light use of the blue pencil, and we're grateful for his helpful revisions and queries. We thank him, too, for his stunning cover design, and we thank N. J. Furl for the attractive interior book design.

Translating takes time from those who are central to our lives. Chen Zeping thanks his wife Weng Zhongyu and Karen Gernant thanks Louis Roemer for their understanding and patience.

Can Xue, meaning "dirty snow, leftover snow," is the pseudonym of Deng Xiaohua. Born in 1953, in Changsha City, Hunan province, her parents were sent to the countryside during the Cultural Revolution, and she only graduated from elementary school. Can learned English on her own and has written books on Borges, Shakespeare, and Dante. Her publications in English include *Dialogues in Paradise*, *Old Floating Cloud*, *The Embroidered Shoes*, *Blue Light in the Sky and Other Stories*, and most recently, *Five Spice Street*.

Karen Gernant, professor emerita of Chinese history at Southern Oregon University, and Chen Zeping, professor of Chinese linguistics at Fujian Teachers' University, collaborate on translating, and more than thirty of their translations have appeared in literary magazines. This is their tenth book.

O pen Letter—the University of Rochester's nonprofit, literary translation press—is one of only a handful of publishing houses dedicated to increasing access to world literature for English readers. Publishing ten titles in translation each year, Open Letter searches for works that are extraordinary and influential, works that we hope will become the classics of tomorrow.

Making world literature available in English is crucial to opening our cultural borders, and its availability plays a vital role in maintaining a healthy and vibrant book culture. Open Letter strives to cultivate an audience for these works by helping readers discover imaginative, stunning works of fiction and by creating a constellation of international writing that is engaging, stimulating, and enduring.

Current and forthcoming titles from Open Letter include works from Argentina, Catalonia, Czech Republic, Poland, Russia, and numerous other countries.

www.openletterbooks.org